# The Awakening

### Killian Verberg

D1665975

# Contents

# Love and Vengeance

FEBRUARY 14, 1986/Camden, Maine

In this world, there are only two pure actions: love, and vengeance.

I've experienced the first only once in my long life. It was a platonic love, a brotherly love, but an intense and fulfilling love nonetheless.

The second? It's intertwined with the first, and will be executed soon.

I bury my hands in the pockets of my blue wool pea coat. Maine is frigid and snowy, so unlike my native Italy. Cold used to bother me, used to chill me to my core, but that was lifetimes ago. Now it's only a minor bother, because I'm tantalizingly close to my mark. What passes as blood in my veins simmers and mixes with my rage.

Fresh snow falls in fat, fluffy flakes, making the little historic downtown here a picture-perfect postcard—and allowing me to go outside in the daytime. Unlike others in my clan, I'm perfectly fine during the day if the sun's not high and bright, so Maine in winter is an excellent assignment for me.

There's something about this place that seems frozen in time, as if it was perpetually stuck in 1946, not 1986. Something stagnant and traditional, provincial and insular.

Today there's a local winter festival, and the streets are packed—or what passes as packed in these parts. Families laughing and eating caramel apples, young couples with feathered hair and intertwined hands, teens in roving packs wearing various shades of neon. It appears the entirety of Camden is here, walking in the middle of Main Street. Vehicles are prohibited for the afternoon, which means it's easy to get lost in the crowd.

This, combined with the gray, sunless sky, makes for perfect hunting.

My targets pause at an ice sculpture. They're about ten feet from me, and I hang back at the next booth, one that's selling postcards and lobster-themed knickknacks. While I pretend to scan the racks, my glance slides to the right.

Thomas and Gabrielle Ransom. They look like any other couple in their sixties here on the coast of Maine. He's wearing a blue fleece jacket, chino pants, duck boots. She's wearing a similar outfit but in red, and her sensible, silver bob is tamed with a matching headband. They look as though they shop frequently at L.L. Bean, where I'd stopped on my way from New York.

I'd even purchased a wool sweater and a pair of boots, figuring I'd need to look the part in this backwater if I ended up at a bar or restaurant. No Armani suits here.

Thomas leans into his wife's ear, whispering something that makes her face light up. She laughs, a sound similar to wind chimes on a breezy day, and rests her hand lightly on his chest. His smile is triumphant, as if it was his life's mission to amuse her.

Fated mates are all the same, the world over. I've seen more than a few in my time, and always found them insipid.

"Um, sir, just to let you know, those are three for a dollar."

I snap my gaze to the young clerk, who has a thick Maine accent and pronounced her last word as dollah. I smile tightly and she beams in response. "Thank you."

"Not a good day for the winter fest, ayuh?" she asks, trying to make small talk. The clerk is about twenty, has long, wheat-colored hair, guileless blue eyes, and a prominent, buck-toothed smile.

I shake my head and quickly select three postcards, not wanting to cause undue attention to myself. Try to blend in. "Could be a little warmer."

"You from around he'ah?"

Her accent is thick in a New England way, and it's unusual to my ear.

"Visiting from New York."

"All that way, wow. We don't get too many outta staters here, at least not in the winter. Most of our tourists left after the leaves changed and fell."

I look deep into her eyes and smile, giving her the full force of my charm. I also lie like a rug. "I'm interviewing for a position at the local academy, so I thought I'd spend the weekend here to get a feel for the quality of life."

She stammers for a moment, obviously pleased. "If you'd like a local guide, I'd be happy to... I mean, if you don't know anyone here, I'd... well, you know."

"That would be lovely."

She opens and closes her mouth several more times. I gently extract a dollar from my wallet and leave it on the counter. "I'm staying at the Hawthorne Inn. Shall we meet tonight at, say, seven? For dinner? Perhaps you can give me the highlights of Camden."

"Yes, of course, oh goodness. I'd love to. I'll see you there, mister.. .what is your name, anyway?"

"Matteo. But you can call me Matt."

I look to my right and notice the Ransoms have shifted. Their backs are now to me, and I worry they're about to walk away. I cannot lose sight of them. Not now.

"Matteo. Oh, whoa. That's an interesting name. Sorry, I'm just nervous, I mean, I don't meet many people from New York. I'm Amy." She babbles some more about her job, or school, or something. I'm not listening.

Instead, I'm focused on Thomas Ransom.

"There she is, my little girl." He stiffly hugs someone, but I can't see who because his sturdy body obscures the person in front of him.

"A pleasure to meet you. I look forward to tonight, Amy." I wink and glide away, scooping up the postcards and slipping them into the interior pocket of my jacket. She will certainly be helpful in my quest, in more ways than one.

But I can't linger. I need to know who Thomas is embracing. I move away from the postcard booth and toward the ice sculptor. There are a handful of people clustered around the artist, who is shaving the block with a sharp, shiny knife.

"Working with the ephemeral really allows me to focus on the process," the bearded sculptor says to no one in particular. Almost everyone nods, and I do too. I'm always mindful of blending in.

Thomas and Gabrielle are only two steps away, but they don't notice me. Their instincts are dulled from years of normalcy, which is unfortunate. Back in his prime, Thomas was one of my kind's most brilliant minds.

Gabrielle air kisses the cheek of the person who was in Thomas's arms.

"You look so pale, Evangeline." Her tone is flat, bored, and accusatory.

I slip around a family wearing bulky, puffer jackets so I can get a better look. My hearing becomes sharper when I hear the name.

Evangeline. The daughter. If she's here, her brother John has to be close by.

Casually, I stand behind the boisterous family, who are now oohing and ahhing over the sculptor, who has taken out a chainsaw.

"It's going to get a little loud," he calls out, as he pulls the cord. The acrid smell of gasoline fills the air, as does the hellacious noise.

I despise sounds like this. Lawnmowers, power tools, motorcycle engines. They all make me edgy and surly.

No one budges, so I can't, either. I slip a few steps back, angling for a view of the girl.

At a faraway booth, the voice of an opera soprano cuts through the noise. For a moment, I'm unsure if I'm hearing an audio hallucination, a moment from my past. I scan the festival, and see that indeed, a local opera company has put someone on a makeshift stage. It's the song Addio del Passato from La Traviata.

The notes, combined with the grind of the chainsaw, bore into my brain. A rush of emotion fills me, remembering that day back in March of 1853 when I saw the premiere in Venice. How that had been the first thing I'd done in years, the first time I'd gone out since Damiano was murdered.

I swallow a mouthful of bile and focus on the task at hand.

Vengeance.

And then, like a shadow, everything around me closes in. I stare at the woman in front of Thomas and Gabriella, and my cold skin prickles.

Her long, red hair is like a blazing sun amidst this gray and white landscape. She's wearing a Victorian-inspired black wool coat, that's nipped at the waist and flared at the bottom. It has fur—perhaps faux, it's hard to tell—around the collar. Everything else on her is black: her gloves, her pants, her boots. Only her face and hair are visible, and her lips are as scarlet as her hair.

This is the Ransom daughter? My research back in Italy must have been faulty, because I thought she was merely a child, years younger than her brother. But what could one expect from only telephone calls and letters? That's why I'm here, in Maine. To find John Ransom myself.

The Council has put its trust in me, and I can't let them down. And of course, this is for Damiano...

"Have you heard from John?" Evangeline asks.

Thomas visibly winces, and Gabrielle's mouth thins.

"He won't be coming. We'll talk about it later. Not here. Not now," Thomas says in a curt, almost rude, tone.

Evangeline sighs and licks her lips, a gesture so alluring, so sensual, that it gives me another idea. Perhaps if I can't find John, I can lure him to me.

With his sister.

AUTHOR'S NOTE: What do you think of Matteo so far?

———

# *Blood Red*

FEBRUARY 23, 1986/Boston, Massachusetts

I'm checking my blood-red lipstick in the mirror and humming along to the sound of The Cure. Hopefully the tape won't snag in the spools again. I swear, we play this album so much that we've worn the cassette out.

Just as I'm swiping a new layer of color on my bottom lip, there's a pounding at my dorm room door.

"Evan, phone call." It's the resident assistant down the hall. "Evan? You in there? I can hear the music. Evangeline?"

I let out an enormous sigh and walk over to the tape player and turn down In Between Days, which is now officially my favorite song. "I'm not here. Not taking calls. Going out."

"It's your mom. Says it's urgent. Says she has some important news."

Rolling my eyes, I turn from the stereo and look to Kerri, my best friend and roommate, who is lounging on her bed, a tiny, dark vision in black. "Just a sec, okay?"

"Be quick. We still need to get a cab and get to Kenmore Square. Traffic's bad tonight because there's a baseball game." She doesn't glance up from admiring her long, black fingernails.

"Coming," I call out while flinging open the door. The RA gives me a long, up-and-down look, and I can tell she doesn't like my outfit. She never does, probably because she dresses like a fifty-year-old preppy woman from Cape Cod in Brooks Brothers and Izod.

"Your mom sounds pissed," the RA says in an accusatory tone.

"That's just her voice," I mutter, but it's probably true. Mom is likely angry about something. My brother, my dad, me. Her job at the psychiatric hospital. Could be anything. My recent visit home to Maine hadn't been a warm, fuzzy family reunion, either. She might still be stewing about that whole fiasco with my brother, who'd conveniently chosen to vanish during Mom and Dad's anniversary weekend.

The pay phone is down the hall, and I strut over, my Docs making heavy, muffled thumps on the worn gray carpeted floor.

"Hi, Mother," I say coolly into the heavy plastic phone receiver.

"I don't even warrant a Mama or a Mom anymore? How interesting. I guess that's a milestone of young adult development." She sighs wearily, although I can detect a hint of edge in her voice. "I guess I should be thankful that I reached you at all."

I'm about to retort with something nasty — just because you're a psychotherapist doesn't mean you can analyze me — but I refrain because Kerri's waiting and I just want to get this phone call over with.

"What's going on?" I can't help but ask, because I'm genuinely curious now. My thumbnail flicks over the grooves of the metal phone cord, and for the millionth time, I wish I had Kerri's nail painting skills.

"They found her."

"Found who?"

Mom sighs again. "Amy Driscoll."

"Oh yeah? Where was she? Did she run away to New York City or something?" I look down the hall and watch Jennifer, a rich trust funder with long, straight blonde hair, emerge from her room. She slams her door, glances to me, sneers, and stalks off like she's walking a runway.

Bitch.

"She was found dead, Evangeline."

The receiver slips from my hand but I catch it before it knocks against the wall. I press it into my ear a little too hard. "What? How? Where?"

Mother clears her throat, a tic she has when she's annoyed. Which is almost always. "Oh, now you're interested in what I have to say."

"Of course I'm interested. I read five newspaper articles about her disappearance when I was at home. Mother, stop being so passive aggressive. What happened to Amy?" During my visit, I rushed outside to get the newspaper each morning, just to get an update on the case. The idea that someone I knew even casually had disappeared was morbidly fascinating to me.

And terrifying, too.

"Her body was found by the Penobscot River, sixty miles north of here. She was murdered. At least that's what police told the paper."

For a second, all I can hear is my breathing. I wasn't friends with Amy, mostly because she was three or four years younger than me. I barely remember her in high school, and only knew any significant details through Mom, who worked with her dad at the hospital.

I'd met Amy only once at the hospital Christmas party last year. She asked me what going to school in Boston was like, and said she couldn't wait to graduate to get the hell out of Maine.

"That's awful, Mom. I'm sorry." My tone softens. "Have they caught the killer?"

"No."

"Her family must be—"

"Evangeline, her neck was ripped open."

Now I stop breathing. There's no sound on the other end of the receiver, and for at least fifteen seconds, Mom and I are silent. Finally, I eke out a reaction. "What?"

"She had no blood in her body, and her jugular was punctured." Another strained round of throat-clearing comes over the line.

I gulp in a breath, then another. "Mom, it can't be what you think it is. It's probably just some psychopath in the woods. Maine's filled with psychopaths. You've read Stephen King. Or it could be an animal. You know that there are bears and cougars and—"

"I don't think a bear drains its victim of blood." Mom's tone is wry.

We both pause, our breathing in tandem as Mom's last sentence hangs in my brain.

"I see," I finally mutter. "Was she assaulted? Sexually?"

"No. Definitely not, according to what the sheriff told me. Regardless, I need you to be careful, young lady. I already don't like how you pal around with that Kerri girl, given who she is."

I push out a sigh because Mom's attitude towards Kerri has always grated on me. Her judgy words, her pinched, strained tone—it's like fingernails on a chalkboard. "Mom, Kerri's harmless. We've had this conversation before."

"None of them are harmless, Evangeline."

"She's my roommate, and she's had plenty of opportunity with me. Nothing's ever happened." Not because I didn't want it to. I'd begged, but Kerri, being a vegan, refused. I don't think her version of veganism is the same as a regular human's, but that's irrelevant for this particular conversation.

Mom makes a hmph sound. "Just be aware of your surroundings. You're twenty-one and I know you're going out to bars and nightclubs and drinking. Don't go home with strange men. Or any men. You've got an excellent future ahead of you, and your father and I don't want you, or anyone else, to ruin it."

"I won't, Mom," I say in a robot-like voice. Inside my body, it feels like my blood is vibrating at her macabre news.

"Please promise me you'll be careful. I... I...," Mom stammers, which is something so unusual that my snarky comeback dries in my throat. "I couldn't stand it if you became one of them. If you became what I used to be."

The bottom line: mom used to be a vampire, and since she turned human, she's against all things vampire. The hypocrisy has never made sense to me. She says she wants to spare me from her experiences as a young woman.

"Mom, please. Things are a lot different now than when you were my age. There were more vampires back then, and they were more violent. Now things are a lot more... organized and safe."

"Tell that to Amy Driscoll. Organized and safe. My goodness." Her breath catches, and for a half-second, I hear a sob. Then she clears her throat. "I'll speak with you tomorrow."

"Okay, Mom. Say hi to Dad."

The click of the receiver and a dial tone replace Mom's tight, tense voice. Other parents might have said an I love you after that difficult conversation. Not my mom. Love is not in her vocabulary.

I go into the shared dorm bathroom to compose myself, wondering if I should tell Kerri about Amy's death. I wash my hands for several long seconds, then look into the mirror to smooth my hair and inspect the perfect smoky shadow that makes my green eyes pop. Tonight, my pale face has pinked-tinged cheeks and my eyes appear unusually bright. Wild, even.

My insides are still quivering from Mom's news, vibrating with excitement, fear, and yes, jealousy.

Because if Mom is right, and Amy Driscoll was attacked by a vampire?

That's the very thing that I long for.

AUTHOR'S NOTE: Okay, okay, I know. This is set in 1986. Which is a LONG time ago. What do you think of the time period in this story?

---

# In Your Dreams

FEBRUARY 21, 1986/Boston, Massachusetts

I'm silent as I watch Kerri smoke. We're standing outside on Beacon Street, waiting for the taxi that will take us to the club. We're a few steps from the entrance to our seven-story dorm that takes up an entire city block. It's a cool, spooky-looking old building, built back in 1901 as a hotel on the edge of Boston Common.

Supposedly it's haunted, but Kerri and I haven't seen any evidence of this. Trust me, we've looked. We've bribed one RA to unlock the door to the basement, found the secret passageway to the staircase on the fourth floor, and have held countless Ouija board sessions.

If we haven't conjured the dead in our four years living in the Charlesgate dorm at Boston University, the dead simply don't exist. Or they want nothing to do with us, which is also a possibility.

"Okay, what's wrong?" Kerri blows a stream of smoke out of her mouth, which is coated in black lipstick. The scent of her clove cigarette mingles with the icy air, creating a unique sweet and spicy smell that I'll probably remember for the rest of my life. I hate smoking, but love the smell of those damned cigarettes.

I shiver and shove my hands inside the sleeves of my black wool coat, wishing I'd worn gloves. "Do I have time to go back upstairs? My hands are freezing."

Kerri sticks the cigarette in the corner of her mouth and fishes around in one of the inside pockets of her black leather jacket. Somehow she's stuffed a pair of gloves in there, and she holds them out. "Here. Now what's going on? You've barely said a word since you took that call from your mom."

I tug on the black leather gloves. They're a little tight on me, because Kerri's so small. "Nothing worth talking about."

"Bullshit. What did Gabrielle Laurentiu Ransom have to say tonight?" Kerri's as skeptical of Mom as Mom is of her. She yawns, as if to say, whatever your mother says is boring as hell.

I angle my body along the stone wall of our dorm building and let out a pained breath. "Mom was calling to tell me about a girl who was found murdered in Maine."

This perks Kerri up. "Did you know her?"

"Vaguely. She's a few years younger than me. But here's the thing." I pause and chew on my bottom lip for a second, wondering what it was like the moment Amy was...taken. Was she afraid? Did she know the power she was about to achieve? Was she ecstatic?

"What? Spit it out, Evan." Kerri has zero patience.

"Her name was Amy, and her body was found by a river, and, uh, you're sure you want to hear this?"

Kerri arches one perfectly groomed black eyebrow. "Do you think I can't handle it?"

I snort out a laugh. "Well, obviously you can."

She takes out another clove cigarette and offers it to me. I shake my head. She lights the cigarette with the one she's smoking, then flicks the old one to the ground.

"It's a good thing you don't have to worry about cancer. I've heard those cloves burn holes in your lungs."

"One of the many perks of being me. Continue." She blows a smoke ring and the shape hangs for a moment in the frigid air before dissolving.

"Fine. Amy's throat was ripped open."

Kerri nods and shifts her gaze away from my face, staring blankly at the empty street. "Probably an animal."

"No. Mom wouldn't have called me if it was an animal. You know what it was. Plus, Mom said the body was drained of blood."

We're interrupted by two guys in ballcaps, sneakers, North Face parkas and shorts who stumble past us on their way inside the dorm. I don't recognize them, probably because they look like every other frat type guy in school. I can, however, smell the beer seeping from every pore. Gah, it's only nine at night, and they're that drunk?

Kerri and I both wrinkle our noses, as if garbage just floated past us.

"Goth chicks are hot," one guy says as he's a few feet past us. "I'd like to bone one."

The second guy turns to grin at us, and I shoot him a withering glare and my middle finger.

Kerri hisses, actually hisses, and flashes her fangs for a millisecond. "In your dreams, ass clown."

The two guys look so panicked that they stumble over each other to get indoors. "Freak," one says.

All I can do is laugh. Whenever she acts like this, rumors spread through the dorm about how she wears fake teeth to complete her perfect goth look. If only they knew.

"Okay, back to your dilemma. What is your dilemma, anyway, baby?" Kerri looks amused, and part of me wants to protest and get huffy. Then again, she's probably tired of my crap. She's heard me drone on about this topic for four long years.

"There's no dilemma."

"Oh but there is. And there's our cab. Excellent timing. But don't think I'll let this go."

A yellow taxi roars up to the curb. We pile in back, where it's cold and smells like—what else—beer. Being in a college town means everything smells like Old Milwaukee on a Saturday night, because the cheap beer is all anyone can afford.

"Axis, 13 Landsdowne," I say through the plastic partition, then slide it shut.

Neither of us bother with seat belts as the driver speeds off.

"Tell me about your issue." Kerri's voice is serious now. "I don't want this to ruin the show tonight. You know how much I adore The Mission. So get it all out. I will not let your funk ruin my time with Wayne Hussey, the hottest lead singer since Jim Morrison. And you know my stories about Jim back in the sixties."

I huff out a laugh. "I'm jealous."

"Of Wayne? Or Jim? You should be jealous of Jim because he ate pu—"

I yelp, which is what I always do when Kerri talks about her past sexual exploits. "Wench. No! Of Amy."

"You're jealous of a murdered girl? Oh Jesus Christ." She rolls her eyes.

"No. Yes. Whatever. Don't make me say it aloud again."

She lets her head flop back against the seat. "Oh God, this again? The immortality crap? You're jealous because a vamp—"

"Shh." I smack her on the leg.

"Hey, careful. These are new tights."

"Yes. I'm jealous because Amy, totally nice, perfectly mediocre Amy, is now going to be immortal. I should be immortal, not her."

Kerri clicked her tongue. "Well, setting aside the fact we don't know that poor Amy will become a living dead girl, I still maintain that immortality isn't as desirable as you think. Shit. Do you want to be like me? I've been an art student, a nurse, a prep cook, a waitress and an assembly line worker making tractors in World War II. It's been a grind for literally a hundred and thirty years. Is that what you want?"

No, I just want to live long enough to develop a cure for one deadly virus. That's all. One lifetime isn't enough for everything I want to do on this planet.

"Why can't you let me decide?" I know my tone sounds petulant, but it always does when it comes to this topic.

"I am letting you decide. If you meet a person willing to turn you, then I'm all in favor of it. Me? I can't go there. I have ethics."

I let out a grunt of air and press my forehead against the window. "I know, and I love you for it. Usually. Tonight I'm not so sure."

Part of me wishes I'd never met Kerri at freshman orientation. Maybe if I hadn't, I would've accepted that I was a half-human, half-vampire, a girl with a foot in both worlds, while living in neither.

Maybe I'd have pledged a sorority, or dressed like a preppy co-ed, or dated normal guys. Maybe I would have forgotten all about my heritage and been normal.

But no, I met Kerri, found a best friend, dress like a goth bride on the regular, and am reminded every day of the one thing I really desire: the freedom to do what I want, for as long as I want.

Death really is a downer, and I don't want to experience it, ever. I've got goals. Plans. Groundbreaking medical ideas, even.

Kerri chuckles, a deep, raspy sound that gives me a glimpse of how old she truly is. "And I love you too, Evan. But I simply can't have you on my conscience for eternity. You're going to have to mature out of this phase and learn to live like a normie. Or find some willing, reckless, and hot vampire to give you what you want."

The taxi driver honks and blows through a yellow light at the intersection of Beacon Street and Massachusetts Avenue. We're almost to the club, and like every night for the past four years that I've gone out in Boston, I hope that tonight, I do find exactly what my best friend just described.

———

AUTHOR'S NOTE: What do you think will happen next?

----

# Embers in Her Eyes

FEBRUARY 21, 1986/Boston, Massachusetts

I swirl the pinot noir around in my glass and turn another page, absorbed in my book. While it's true that I'm a two hundred-year-old, opera-loving, highbrow culture-consuming, occasionally violent immortal, I have exactly one guilty pleasure.

Romantic fiction.

Yes, yes, I know I said I deeply disliked fated mates. But only in real life. Fictional happiness is somehow far more satisfying, at least to me. Probably this is due to my occupation as a young man, during the time that I was human. I was a poet for several years.

Over the decades I've been a voracious consumer of popular books, bestsellers, and now, romance. It's always been a way to escape the tedium of my existence. Writing has eluded me since I was turned into this current form, and it's one of my chief frustrations about my life.

Or what passes as a life.

Damiano would laugh his ass off if he saw me tonight, a muscular, angry-eyed vampire reading a romance novel in an expensive home in Boston. If he'd lived, he would've wanted to stroll down the hill to the Ritz and sit at the bar, hoping to pick up some gorgeous socialite and then drink her blood while giving her the best orgasm of her life.

Once upon a time, I was like that with women.

These days, all the eroticism I need is in books, because humans bore me. I especially enjoy the historical romances set in Europe in the nineteenth century; it's always fascinating to see how the fictional world compares with my own experience.

Tonight I'm inhaling something a little different: Jackie Collins' Lucky. It's one of the biggest books of this decade, and while I'm not a fan of the prose, I have to say the Mafia plot is addicting, like a sexier Godfather. It's a campy and fun book, and probably far more interesting than what I have to deal with later tonight.

I finish the chapter and set the book down on a dark mahogany end table. There's a sip of wine left in the glass, but I don't touch it. Instead, I check my vintage Rolex, then slip it off my wrist and set it on top of the book. Ten o'clock. I click off a lamp, and bright moonlight streams into the room, casting beautiful shadows on one of the exposed brick walls.

It's time to leave the cool, quiet sanctuary of this Beacon Hill home and go in search of my prey. A dark nightclub is the perfect setting for what I need to do this evening.

Fortunately, my stalking this past week paid off. It hadn't taken much to pay off an intern in the registrar's department at Boston

University. That young woman had given me Evangeline Ransom's entire schedule. Then, I'd lingered outside of a lecture hall, and fell into lockstep behind her and another woman.

They'd talked excitedly about an upcoming concert at a club called Axis. Some band called The Mission was playing. I'd never heard of them, but that wasn't surprising. I was familiar with fiction trends, not music.

I'd had to do a little asking around on campus about The Mission. One guy with a pierced nose and a mohawk had called them "rad," and another girl with pale skin and black lipstick said they were "goth." Eventually I'd been forced to walk to Tower Records on Massachusetts Avenue to buy an album.

To my surprise, they weren't bad.

I throw a leather jacket over my plain black T-shirt. I've also decided to wear black jeans and leather Doc Marten boots, since that's what I've seen men wear around the city. Over the decades, I've become an expert in blending in.

The frigid air outside doesn't bother me, and I light a cigarette while hailing a cab on Charles Street. The driver wants to make small talk, but I respond in monosyllabic grunts. I've never understood Americans' need to be pleasant.

At the club, I stuff a fifty into the cabbie's hand through the window—while I can be an asshole, I'm not a stingy tipper—and saunter to the club entrance. I'd bought VIP tickets, and apparently that means I can skip the long line that snakes around the block.

Once inside, my eyes immediately adjust to the dark club, and I head straight to the bar. Everyone's drinking beer, which I normally loathe. Irritated, I order a Rolling Rock, which is what every other man is drinking here.

Bottle in hand, I rest my bicep against a back wall and survey the club. On the stage at the front of the room, roadies arrange guitars and microphones. The crowd's voices drown out the rock music playing over the sound system.

It's a cavernous place, heavy with the scent of Dior's Poison perfume, and it's packed with people. Many of them women. How in the hell will I ever find Evangeline Ransom here, in this sea of people dressed in head-to-toe black? I scan the crowd for a head of bright red hair. Fortunately, she'll stand out with those long, flaming tresses.

"Come here often?"

A female voice slices through my concentration. I turn to my right, fully aware of the murderous look in my eyes.

"I've never been here in my life."

The woman grins, probably thinking I'm a challenge. She's in a long, angular blazer with shoulder pads. Black, of course. I think she's wearing only black stockings underneath, with pointy boots. Her hair's messy and spiky. Black, like the shadow that lines her eyes. "Cool. It's going to be an amazing show."

"I expect so. I quite like their first album." I nod and take other swig of my beer.

"It sounds like you're not from Boston. You have a different accent." She smirks.

"Italy."

"Oh. Are you a student?"

I shake my head but don't offer more information about myself. "You?"

"I go to BU."

I can't help but grin at my good fortune. "You wouldn't happen to know an Evangeline Ransom, would you? I'm supposed to meet her here."

Disappointment flashes in her eyes for a second. "Name sounds familiar. What's she look like?"

"Red hair." I pause. "Pretty. Extremely pretty. And short. Maybe this tall. She really loves this band."

I hold my free hand up to my shoulder.

"Pre-med? I think I know her. She was in my anthropology class last semester."

"Oh? You see her tonight?"

She scans the crowd, then points toward the stage as she presses herself against me. She's warm, a fact that has never ceased to surprise me about humans over the years. I was once like that as well, I guess.

"There. See? To the left of the stage? Next to the girl with the short, spiky hair and the leather jacket with studs?"

My gaze lands on a shock of red hair. Evangeline Ransom.

"Yes, that's her," I say softly.

Evangeline turns to the woman with the spiky hair and I can see her in profile now. She's more confident looking tonight than when I first spotted her in Maine. How interesting.

"Thank you," I say to the woman next to me.

"Want me to walk down there with you?" She brushes her breast against my arm.

I step away. "Thank you, but no. I'm going to grab another drink first, then go to her. Have fun at the show."

Thankfully she doesn't follow me as I dissolve into the crowd. I do a lap around the room, throw away my disgusting beer, and slowly work my way through the crowd on the dance floor. Evangeline and her friend have edged closer to the stage, standing among a cluster of people.

I keep my eyes fixed on her red hair as I move toward her, gripping my beer as I go. I slip past two guys with shaved heads and finally, I'm behind her. Close enough to reach out and touch her pale neck.

She's even shorter than I thought, but the thing that instantly intrigues me is her fire-colored hair. It's long, wavy, and flows over her shoulders and down her back. Perhaps it's dyed.

I shoot a glance at her companion, needing to know what I'm up against if I want to get Evangeline alone. I've heard that American girls are reluctant to let their friends leave bars with strange men, but I have yet to confirm that myself.

Evangeline and her friend are swaying a little to the recorded music coming over the speakers. They're both drinking from plastic cups—bless them for not swilling beer, how unattractive for women—and the friend downs hers.

"Want another?" She leans over to yell in Evangeline's ear, which means I can hear every word.

The friend's eyes flicker to me. After all, I'm standing only a foot away, since we're all packed in here like sardines. Then she grins, and that's when I see them.

Her fangs.

Well. This is an interesting development. Little Evangeline Ransom's friend is a vampire. I wonder if her brother is aware of this.

"Yeah, get me another. Cranberry and vodka," Evangeline yells back.

"Okay. Don't let anyone take my place. And be careful. There are some real creeps here." The friend shoots me another knowing look and lurches through the crowd. I wonder what clan she's from, and whether she knows what—or who—I am.

I have to work fast.

Evangeline stops her dancing just as the two skinheads I'd passed earlier slide into the space where the friend was standing.

"Hey. That spot's taken," Evangeline says, turning to them. Her profile is so damned pretty. Such a shame she's related to my sworn enemy.

"I don't see anyone standing here," the taller of the two says.

"C'mon. Don't be a dick," Evangeline retorts. "My friend was just here, she's getting our drinks."

"What does she look like? Maybe she'll want to share our space." The guy eyes Evangeline lasciviously and I instantly want to kill him. "Why don't you get nice and close to me?"

The guy winks, which makes me clench my hand into a fist. There's nothing I love more than beating the shit out of skinheads. Or worse...

Evangeline hauls in a breath, obviously exasperated. She knows that if she protests further, the guy's attitude will get even worse.

She turns a half step and faces me, her jaw clenched and tense. We lock eyes and I feel a zing shoot through me. The crowd and the noise fall away for a second, and I can only focus on those eyes, a clear blue like the sky in Tuscany.

I wonder what words, what ideas, what poetry, those eyes hold within.

The corner of her scarlet mouth quirks up.

Unable to help myself, I lean down, into her ear and speak in a low growl. "Do you need my help?"

She nods and squeezes my arm. "Please, and thank you."

Her little whisper sends a shiver through my body.

"Amore mio," I say loudly while glaring at the guys, "Are these two assholes giving you a hard time?"

"Yes. They are. Kerri went to get us drinks while you were in the bathroom and they refuse to move." She presses herself against me, and I slide an arm around her shoulders. She's the perfect actress, with an adorable pout on those scarlet lips.

She's close enough that I can detect her perfume. My sense of smell is sharp, and I inhale marshmallow and vanilla in the beginning, then a darker, sultry musk in the base note. Sweet and delicious, heady and mysterious. I like it.

A lot.

"Get the fuck out of here," I growl at the guy closest to Evangeline. He's big, but not as big as me.

"You gonna make me?" he says, puffing his chest. He's wearing a ridiculous T-shirt with some sort of anarchist symbol on it, and I want to spit on him because I actually fought with the original anarchists in Italy back in the late 1800s. Poser.

His friend eyes me and reaches for his buddy's bicep. I get the distinct feeling that they're more than a little familiar with my kind.

"Dude. No. You don't want to go there. C'mon, there's a couple of girls on the other side of the stage. Let's go."

Anarchist T-shirt guy shoots me a glare and flings off his friend's hand with a wave of his arm, then stomps away.

"Sorry," his friend says quickly to Evangeline. "He's a little drunk."

She gives him a sour look but doesn't move from my side. We both watch as the guys strut off in their heavy boots. They shove a smaller guy out of their way.

"Charming," I murmur, wishing I could bash their heads in simply for that.

Evangeline slowly steps out of my embrace and exhales. "Thanks. That could've gotten ugly."

"My pleasure."

"I hate men like that."

"So do I."

We stare at each other for a beat. There's something about this woman that I can't put my finger on. Something unusual. And it's not just because her brother is the one who's trying to eradicate my kind.

It's as if she has embers in her eyes and fire in her veins.

This woman, this situation, this night. It's going to be complicated, I can already tell.

"I'm Evangeline," she says.

"Matteo."

As if on cue, the lights in the place dim to near-blackness, and the drums thunder, loud enough that I can feel the sound in my heart. A blaze of light illuminates the stage, and the raven-haired singer runs out to grab the microphone. Evangeline still hasn't turned around to face the band, and all I can see is her gorgeous face and all that red hair.

For the first time in decades, there's a stir of longing and desire coursing through my body. Or is that because I'm one step closer to revenge? I don't have time to figure it out, because she's coming closer. Much to my delight.

She stands on her tiptoes, leaning into me, trying to reach my ear. I oblige by tilting my head and gently clasping her arm.

"I'll buy you a beer after the first set, okay?" She flashes me a saucy grin then whirls around, sending a wave of sweet, floral fragrance my way.

Maybe this won't be so complicated after all.

———

AUTHOR'S NOTE: Hmmm. Thoughts on the two of them?

———

# Ache

FEBRUARY 21, 1986/Boston, Massachusetts

This singer's voice is laced with a romantic huskiness that reverberates through my veins, tugging at some invisible, needy part of me. It makes me want to do wicked things, to chuck my carefully constructed life into the garbage.

Or maybe that's just the acute awareness of being inches away from a man with the most intense blue eyes I've ever seen. It's a feeling of desire, a sharp, visceral attraction. What I want is to turn and kiss him, to do something totally out of character for me. To follow my desire for once.

But I won't. I'm way too timid, especially with guys I'm interested in. Still, the way he defended me against those skinhead jerks was so freaking hot. And I did promise to buy the guy a beer. That was bold, at least for me.

I glance around at the crowd, hoping to see Kerri pushing through with our beers. My eyes alight on a tall woman with black, spiky hair who's standing next to the stage. Oh, there's Kerri. She's worshiping the lead singer, swaying without a care in the world, screaming her head off. Wait, is she blowing kisses at the singer? Yes, she is. I laugh out loud while watching her.

Since Kerri doesn't have our drinks in her hands—those are in the air, extended toward the singer—I figure she hasn't even gone to the bar yet. She's too enamored with that singer, and I know for a fact that she's been hoping to meet, and fuck, him.

There's that desire thing again.

It comes easy to Kerri. Everything does. As a hundred-and fiftysomething-year-old vampire, she's had plenty of practice. She's perfected everything on her own, from enrolling in college to getting a job at a blood bank so she always has a fresh supply of food, to seducing men to sate her sexual desires. She's independent to her core, and I worship her.

Me? I haven't mastered shit. Even though I've been a straight-A student ever since I started kindergarten, I still feel like I'm not living up to my full potential. Kerri chalks this up to my age and type-A behavior, but I know better.

It's because I've been surrounded by uniquely accomplished and incredibly brilliant people my entire life.

Take my parents, for example.

They were once vampires. Dad was born in Romania and was turned hundreds of years ago by Dracula himself. Mom is younger, only about a hundred years old, and from New York. She became a vampire when she was bitten by a jazz singer at the age of twenty-four.

She and dad met in the city at some poetry reading in the early sixties; back then, she was attending school to become a psychotherapist and dad was a celebrated English professor. Once they got together, they immediately knew they were soul mates—and promptly had my brother, and then me.

A stupid decision, in my opinion. In our particular vampire clan, once soul mates give birth to a child, they become mortal. They age like any other human, and they die.

The child is born a half-vampire, half-human. While us halfling children have some vampire traits— such as sharp intelligence, a fine-tuned sense of smell, and heightened intuition—we're still mortal. Which means we age and die like any ordinary human.

The ageing part doesn't bother me at all; I don't fear wrinkles or gray hair. It's the death thing that's the problem (Kerri laughed at me when I first said this).

When I was thirteen and staring at the stars one night at our summer home, a frightening thought occurred to me: I was going to die. Maybe not soon, but someday.

It seemed supremely unfair, especially considering that I had a heritage of immortality.

A normal lifespan isn't enough time to do all I want—namely, find a cure for a virus that kills vampires. It started killing our kind in the 1700s in Europe and has circulated ever since.

Perhaps my obsession with my ancestry, my vampire heritage, is why I've wanted to befriend them. Kerri was my first true vampire friend. There was also another cool girl our sophomore year, but Anya graduated from Boston University and moved to Hollywood to work as a journalist.

I've also met a few vampire guys since coming to college in Boston—my home state of Maine isn't exactly vampire central—but Kerri's always vetted and vetoed them, saying that I don't want to be turned by "just any blood sucking fuck boy."

Kerri's probably right, and that's why I'd begged her to turn me. She refuses, though, saying I'll eventually regret it. She says I should just get laid with a regular, human guy instead. Lose my virginity to some hot punk guy.

I glance at her again, and I can see her fully, her face in profile from where I'm standing. Somehow she's taken off her leather jacket and is only in a thin, black tank top. She's dancing with her eyes closed, swaying as if she's been hypnotized by the music.

Maybe she's right. Maybe I need to let loose for once and embrace my human side. Accept my desires. But that leaves me feeling emptier than ever, since my one desire is immortality. I can feel the march of time with each month that passes. Hell, this is my last year of undergraduate, and in September, I'm scheduled to start medical school at the university here.

Life goes by so fast.

I move a little to the beat, trying to mimic Kerri. Probably I look like a robot, or if I'm lucky, one of those women in Robert Palmer's

Addicted to Love video. Trying to be casual, I slowly turn, pretending to look for someone so I can check out the guy with hot blue eyes again. Matteo. That's his name. So sexy.

He's directly behind me, so close that I can smell the leather of his jacket. He grins, a lazy, lopsided smile. Then he leans toward me. "Your friend's not back yet?"

I shake my head and sway to the music.

"You want a drink?" he asks.

I shake my head again.

Matteo raises a dark eyebrow. Holy crap, this guy is handsome. Not in a traditional way, but in a brutal, masculine way. He looks different than most guys my age, probably because his shoulders are broad and muscular. His jaw is a little too sharp and square, his flashing blue eyes are a little too cold.

There's something beyond his looks that's unsettling, but I can't put my finger on it. I'm both repelled and wildly attracted to him, and I don't understand any of what I'm feeling in this moment. All I know is that I don't want to turn around and look at the band—I want to stand here and stare at him for hours.

He leans in again to speak. The music's so loud he has to put his mouth against my ear, and the sensation makes little explosions go off in my brain and shower through my body.

"What do you want, Evangeline?" He has an accent, but I can't place it. The tone is foreign and sultry, heavy and low, and I want to indulge in more of it.

He pulls back and stares into my eyes. We're standing still in a sea of swaying people, while the music and the aroma of clove cigarettes and marijuana swirl around us. We're only about six inches apart, and I realize I'm breathing heavily. Panting, almost. I don't quite understand what this man is doing to me, or why I'm so affected. Those five words he just uttered seemed to tug at that same place the music did, as though something dark and delicious was pulling my insides tight.

What do I want?

Him. I'm dying for a kiss. I'm tired of playing it safe.

I lean up and press my lips to his. He responds by wrapping a possessive arm around my waist and hauling me into his body, consuming me with his mouth. Oh. Whoa. He's serious with this kiss. It's a kiss that makes me forget everything. Med school, my difficult mother, the fact that we're standing in a crowd at a concert.

Every part of me aches, but most of all, that spot between my legs, the one I've never told anyone about. The one I touch in the dead of night, silently and filled with longing.

His other hand slides along my neck, partially trapping my hair between his fingers.

"This is what you want?" he murmurs against my mouth, and I almost spontaneously combust from how erotic it sounds.

"Y-yes," I stammer, breathless and probably unattractively geeky. I can feel my cheeks alight with heat, and I press myself against his hard body. Now that I'm close to him, I can not only smell the leather of his jacket, but a subtle scent on his skin. I detect hints of gunpowder and smoke, of a spicy incense and a twinge of a scarlet rose. It translates into an edgy darkness that I want to explore, but one that also makes me afraid of what I'm getting into.

"Fuck," he whispers, then goes in for another hard kiss. I catch a glimpse of his eyes, and before he lowers those long, dark lashes, I see a flash of red in his pupils. I gasp lightly, but either he doesn't hear, or doesn't pay attention, because he's still kissing as if he wants to consume me.

Maybe he does.

When he nips my bottom lip with sharp teeth, a thrilling thought flashes through my mind.

Matteo is a vampire.

———

AUTHOR'S NOTE: Is Evan being too reckless? Hmm.

———

# Kiss the Night

FEBRUARY 21, 1986/Boston, Massachusetts

We stand there and kiss for what seems like forever, blocking everything out around us. The band, the people, the smell of the clove cigarettes mixed with the acrid fake fog coming off the stage—it's all muted and hazy. The music, loud and droning with heavy beats, surrounds us and seems to pound in time with my heartbeat.

What am I doing? I've never kissed a guy at a club. It's only been in the last year that I even go to clubs, and that was because Kerri had encouraged me to get out of the library and stop studying.

I don't know anything about this man. His last name, his school, his favorite band. He's a complete stranger and yet I'm throwing myself at him as if he's my last salvation, the only one who can keep me alive. All because of his kisses that are punishing yet seductive, commanding yet languid. Like we have all the time in the world to keep kissing here in the middle of this concert.

And worse, I want more. A twinge of shame twists in my gut, but forbidden lust wins out.

Matteo doesn't stop, and neither do I. We kiss and kiss, unable to get enough of each other. I'm usually reserved and shun male attention, except when guys work hard to get to know me. Even then, I'm fairly selective; Mother's admonishment to only get to know nice boys has always echoed in my mind.

The few guys I've dated in college, they've always approached me with reverence, hesitation, and sometimes, I let them in. But never too much—never all the way sexually—and never this soon. Never in this kind of public place; normally I'd be too shy and embarrassed.

But with Matteo, this stranger who might, possibly, could be a vampire (if my instincts are correct), I'm pouring my soul into this kiss. Pouring my heart into his flesh. In between songs, in the seconds that the band is quiet, a couple of people nearby make a loud, snide comment but we ignore them, because right now, this kiss is all that matters. My body's pressed into his and my arms are around his neck, while his hands are clasping my jaw with enough force that I can't move much.

I'm ignoring everything Mother has warned me—especially since there's a chance he might be a vampire. The more I kiss him the more I'm certain of this fact. His cool flesh in this now-steamy club, the eyes that flash scarlet for a millisecond when he seems to be hyper-aroused, the way he keeps trailing his nose and lips over my jugular on my neck. He feels foreign, and not just because he has an accent of some sort.

"You smell so fucking incredible. I've never smelled this scent before," he says, almost to himself, as his lips linger on the sensitive skin above my collarbone.

Can he smell my blood rushing through my veins? Oh, God, I hope so, as much as the idea terrifies me if he's what I think he is. I want him to lose control and take me, to fulfill my dream once and for all. Let's get this over with...

All signs point to vampire with Matteo. Plus I have a sixth sense that can detect these things, and alarm bells are going off in my brain like they've never done before. The warnings are to stay away, but my fucked-up-priorities are telling me to forge ahead and damn the consequences, no matter what.

If he's truly a vampire, he would be the worst man of all, according to Mother, a race to be avoided at all costs. She's never really explained why, just said doesn't want me to end up like her, faced with the decision to stay immortal or love a soul mate and have a child and become like everyone else. I've never been able to figure out what she feels is a worse fate, but I know what I'd choose, and it's not the husband and kids and mortality.

No, she would tell me to run out of this club, run far from his dark stubble that's scratching my chin to ribbons, run from his kisses that consume me, run from his spicy scent that surrounds me and makes me weak in the knees.

But I don't want to. Quite the opposite. I want more, like a starving woman in a desert. I want everything he can possibly give me, especially the immortality part. And if he's a mere human?

That's fine, too, I guess. Because I'm sick of being the good girl and he's stupidly sexy. What would it hurt to hook up with him? I've never done that during my four years in college, and in a few short months I'm starting medical school.

Of course, there's the specter of AIDS, which has been in the papers lately. But that's what condoms are for, right? Well, that and preventing the unthinkable: children.

For a moment, he pauses and inhales away from my mouth. His eyes slightly roll back into his head as if he can't quite grasp what's happening here, either. Or maybe he's trying to summon some inner control. Then he wraps his fingers around my wrist and tugs roughly, pulling me through the crowd.

"But, but... Kerri," I protest. He doesn't hear me, and I allow myself to be led through the thicket of people, all dancing and swaying to the drumbeat of goth rock.

Where are we going? Out of the club? I need to tell Kerri that I'm leaving. I can't allow her to be alone. It doesn't matter that she's strong enough to take care of herself. We have a pact: never leave a friend behind.

She's always more concerned about me—when we went to a club called Narcissus last month, I'd had a bit too much to drink and started to sloppily dance and make out with some townie from Revere. She'd pulled me away and back to the dorm, saying that I didn't want to "go there" with a "guy like that."

But tonight, I'll go anywhere with this dark and mysterious man. It feels dangerous, yes, but also puzzlingly perfect. And if he can turn me into a vampire—give me what I want—then I want him even more.

Once we reach the edge of the crowd I spot the illuminated sign for the exit, but instead, he yanks me right, toward a long, dark corridor that led to the bathrooms. Interesting. Why doesn't he want to leave? Where is he taking me?

Since the band is well into its first set the corridor is empty, save for a couple of people stumbling to and from the bathroom, probably to do a few lines of coke. That means the dark hallway, with its black-painted walls, is secluded.

Still with that possessive grasp of my wrist, he leads me half way down the hall, between the two bathroom doors. Once we arrive at a smooth patch of black-painted stone wall, he stops and presses me against the wall.

His motion is so hard that my breath catches in my throat, out of fear and sheer lust.

His hands slide over my jaw, spanning my neck, and he brings his face to mine. "We needed a more private place for what I want to do to you," he mutters, before he assaults my mouth.

He kisses me again, but it's nothing like those first kisses on the dance floor. This is ravenous, hungry, fierce. I try to match his intensity but eventually give up, because he desires something I'm unable to comprehend. And the less I try to mimic him, the more he seems aroused.

"Do you like this?" He murmurs against my mouth.

I can only gasp and nod in agreement.

"Don't lie to me," he says.

"I'm...I'm not."

"Good girl." A surge of pure lust makes me shiver at his words.

He pauses, inching back as if to appraise me. His eyes are filled with lust but something else. Scrutiny, perhaps. As if he's sizing me up. Wondering if I'm worthy of him. I don't feel like I am, but desperately want to be.

"This is probably a terrible idea," he says, reaching to stroke my cheek.

My eyes, which had been half lidded with desire, open wide. "Why?"

He shakes his head and kisses me again, which sends a fresh shock wave of need through me, setting a flame directly from my lips right to my stomach and lower. No, I've never felt like this when kissing any of the guys I'd met at a college. This is as if my insides are on fire, and the problem is, I'm not sure if more kisses with Matteo will quench that heat.

Our kisses turn slow and deep, while ripple after ripple of desire flows through me. It's a moment that feels as though it will define my entire life, as if it as outsize meaning. Or perhaps I'm tipsy, or emotional, or...

"You're fucking beautiful, Evangeline." He lets out a low growl, something only I can hear.

Never has a man spoken to me this way, with a mixture of reverence and desperation in his voice. It makes me feel both vulnerable and powerful and I don't know how to answer. So I pull him closer to me, so I can attempt, in my own feeble way, to show him.

We kiss for the length of three more songs. A delicious eternity, one that makes me feel like I'm getting to know him with every nip of his teeth, with every shared breath. He traps my wrists in his hands and holds them above my head.

"You're a perfect kisser, you know that?" he says.

I didn't, but all I can do is lick my lips in response. My mouth feels bruised, raw, from his touch.

"You're not even nervous, are you, Evangeline?"

"I am," I whisper.

"Nervous about what?" He casually smooths my hair back, as if he's been doing it for years.

"I don't know. You. This is so...weird."

"Me?" A little smile creeps on his lips.

"You're... different."

He chuckles, a low, languid sound. As he does this, he draws me in for a hug that's shockingly intimate. This is confusing my senses, because up until now, our interaction has been based on lust. "This is weird? Or good?"

He smiles, but it's not the most reassuring expression. It's more feral, dangerous.

"Weird and good. Scary."

"Why? Because I make you feel something?"

I nod, still unsure, and he moves in with a smirk, planting a soft kiss on my mouth that turns my insides into molten lava, thick and hot. What is happening to me? Holy crap. I am feeling more than I usually do, am shocked out of my usual numb autopilot that propels me through classes and studying and visits with my parents.

"What do I make you feel, Evangeline?"

I'm about to answer in a stream of consciousness—turned on, excited, wet, horny, terrified, anxious—when the shriek of a female voice hits my ears.

"So that's where you went. Evan? Hey!"

It's Kerri, and Matteo and I both turn our heads. His hand is deep in my hair, which is tangled and messy, and he lets go of me with a soft groan.

I giggle nervously. "Hey Kerri, uh, this is Matteo."

She looks him up and down. "Hi. Took me long enough to find you. Are you leaving?"

"We're headed back to her dorm in a few minutes," Matteo says casually.

An alarm bell goes off in my head. How does he know I live in a dorm? Sure, Boston is a college town, and lots of people live in dorms. But still.

Kerry reaches for me and yanks me out of his embrace. We stand a few feet away from Matteo, and she presses her mouth into my ear and yells. I can smell the beer leaking from her every pore.

"I'm not sure about this. Are you okay?"

"I'm fine," I say.

"I think you should come with me back to the stage." Her face is pinched with worry, the shadows and prisms of the stage lights bouncing off her pale skin.

I shake my head. "I want this. I want him."

She fixes a stony gaze at me. "I get a bad vibe from him."

I dismiss her with a wave of my hand. "He's harmless."

"Bullshit. You know exactly what he is." Kerri has a far more developed vampire radar than I do, for obvious reasons.

"Let me do what I want," I hiss.

"You're not going to let this go, are you? What if I drag you kicking and screaming away from him? What if I told you the bassist of the band is hot and probably even more willing than mystery man over here?"

"No, Kerri. Not interested." Silently I shoot her a glare. If she'd turn me into a vampire, none of this would be happening. But she won't. Won't accept that responsibility of turning a half-human into an undead creature. Apparently there's some taboo or law against that in vampire culture, but it's not a big deal, as far as I'm concerned. It's my body, my choice.

"You're going to do what you want, and I can't to stop you. God knows no one could stop me." She holds my face in her hands. "I just don't want to have to clean up his mess, your mess, if things go wrong."

"So far he's only done things right, if you know what I mean. Honestly, I think it's just sex. That's really what I want. I think."

She huffs out a laugh. "Spoken like a true virgin. Listen, go back to the dorm. Do not go to his house or dorm or apartment. Go to a familiar place. I'll be there in a while. Try not to do anything I wouldn't do."

I let out a genuine giggle. "That doesn't leave out much," I say.

She grabs my arm. "You know what to do if things get out of control, right?"

I nod. Once, when I met a vampire guy last year and thought he'd be the one to turn me, she showed me exactly how to repel him if I felt the situation wasn't right. She'd instructed me to buy and hide a large silver cross in our room, and made me promise me not to show it to her — but that I should feel free to flash the religious relic at any out-of-control vampire guy that I met. I'd never had the chance with the guy from last year, because he'd ghosted me without explanation, vanished without a trace.

Vampires, and vanishing vampires, weren't uncommon in Boston. They moved among the humans seamlessly, so I wanted to always be prepared. I'd never had to use it, because I'd never gotten that close to a vampire who wanted to take me to bed—or to turn me.

The ornate silver cross is stashed under my mattress, just in case. "You also be careful," I say. It's unnecessary, of course, because she has superhuman strength. Just one more reason I want to be like her.

"Pfft. I've already been invited backstage to meet the band. The bodyguard approached me and asked me to hang out with the band. You sure you don't want to join me? It's going to be fucking insane."

I shake my head. Musicians aren't my thing. Mysterious, dark-haired, sharp-jawed strangers are, apparently.

She wanders off, consumed by the crowd near the stage. I turn back to Matteo, who's casually leaning against a wall as if he couldn't be bothered with any of my stupid college conversations. I half expect him to roll his eyes, but he doesn't. Instead, he stares with those blue eyes, all intense and sexy, and I adore him even more.

"Want to get pizza in Kenmore Square? Or go back to my dorm and talk?" I ask.

He grins, an expression so wicked and decadent that I almost run after Kerri. Can I handle this man? There's no turning back now. Whatever is about to happen, will happen, and it's as if I can't change the course of fate.

"Lead the way, beautiful. Not interested in pizza, and I want more from you than conversation."

As he clasps my hand tight and we walk into the frigid Boston night that slaps me in the face with its bracing temperature, thrilling tingles shower through my body.

This might be the moment I've hoped for my entire life.

——

AUTHOR'S NOTE: Whatever could Matteo want from her?

——

# A Punishing Kiss

FEBRUARY 21, 1986/Boston, Massachusetts

Of all the things I expected from this evening, this wasn't among them.

I thought I'd go to the club, watch Evangeline, make eye contact, maybe buy her a drink. Engage in small talk, charm her into giving me her number. Lay the groundwork for using her to lure her brother out of hiding.

I didn't expect that she'd press her curvy, gorgeous body against mine. Didn't anticipate she'd kiss me with such passion, such ferocity, that a long-dormant spark would alight in my chest. Didn't think I'd feel my first twinge of lust in decades.

"My dorm's not far. We can take a taxi, or walk. Kerri and I took a taxi to the club, because it's still pretty cold."

We're hand in hand, walking down a dark Boston street. I won't let go of her because of the men that lurk in the shadows and alleys. At best, they look like human trash, dregs that would devour petite

Evangeline in a second. At worst, they look like underworld thugs that would devour her in a different way.

Probably to the drunk college students staggering past, those men of the underworld probably seem like bikers, or drug dealers, or random tough guys. The kind of men that humans overlook every day. I know better. Given Evangeline's background, I wonder if she does, as well.

Regardless, she's mine for tonight. The question is, what am I going to do with her?

"The dorm's down this street, then to the left." She points ahead of us. "How did you know I lived in the dorm, anyway?"

Her voice slices through my thoughts and the icy Boston air. We've rounded a corner and are headed toward Kenmore Square, a seedy part of town that seems to cater to American baseball fans and punk rockers, if the people with mohawks flowing into a bar called The Rathskeller are any indication.

I squeeze Evangeline's hand. "Educated guess. Doesn't everyone in Boston live in dorms."

She stops in front of the bar and stares into my face, tilting her head so her red hair spills over her shoulder. "Where do you live, Matteo?"

Her green eyes are so beautiful that I can't help but lean in for a kiss. One more thing I didn't anticipate: that I enjoy kissing her. So very odd.

"You didn't answer me," she murmurs against my mouth, then giggles.

Out the corner of my eye I spot several shady-looking guys in black, smoking outside the club. They eye me cautiously, and look to Evangeline with interest. Of course they do; she stands out with that long, red mane and her gorgeous face. I idly wonder if she wanders around here at night on her own, and a brief shudder flows through me.

I tug Evangeline away. Not that I couldn't fight a pack of undesirables on my own.

"I'm a bit of a nomad." That's a good hedge, perhaps.

"So you don't have a home?"

I let out a chuckle. "Having second thoughts about me?"

"I don't bring just any homeless guy back to my dorm, you know. You're special."

"My home is in Italy."

There's a pause, and I suspect she's working through the logistics of all this in her mind. "So why are you here in Boston? And for how long? Are you a student?"

We walk under a highway overpass, the darkness enveloping us. She edges closer to me, and out of instinct, I let go of her hand and slide my arm around her shoulders. The cars whizzing past don't drown out the crackling sexual tension I feel between us.

"I'm in town on business. I'm here for a few weeks, maybe a month. Just arrived the other day."

"I see. You seemed like you could be a graduate student, but too old for undergrad."

I know she's fishing for my age, but I don't want to go down that particular road. "And you? How about you?"

"Senior at Boston University. Pre-med. Just turned twenty-one last month. I've been accepted to BU's medical school, and I start in the fall."

"Impressive. What kind of medicine do you want to practice? Do you know yet?"

She flashes me a smile. "I'm interested in virology. The study of viruses."

Her answer makes me feel as if I have ice freezing in my veins. Is her choice of study a coincidence? Does she know more about her heritage than I expected? Her ancestor was the man who developed the deadly virus that killed my best friend—and thousands of other vampires across the globe—and her brother is the evil bastard trying to resurrect that research to kill us all.

What if she's in on her brother's plan?

"Interesting," I say, trying to keep the distaste out of my mouth. "Any particular reason you chose that?"

"I've always been fascinated by infectious disease." She laughs, a genuine, beautiful sound. Or it would be beautiful if my anger wasn't rising like the bile in my throat. "That sounds weird, doesn't it?"

I'm about to answer when she pipes up.

"There's my dorm."

It's a big, brick structure, gothic-looking and imposing. We cross the street and she slips out of my embrace as we walk up the steps and pass through the glass doors. There's a young guy sitting behind a desk just inside. He's watching a small black and white TV that's blaring one of those obnoxious comedies with the laugh track.

"Hey, Alex," she says, gesturing at me. "He's my guest. What are you watching tonight?"

"Perfect Strangers. It's hilarious." He beams at her.

Alex, who seems quite enamored with Evangeline, eyes me warily. "Sign into the book, 'kay?"

I glance down at the open red binder, grab the pen and scrawl my name. Evangeline watches with interest.

"Matteo Moretti," she murmurs.

I smirk at her, still unable to get the memory of my best friend's gruesome, painful death out of my mind. Her family caused that. I cannot forget.

"Have a good night, Alex," she trills, then turns to me, her eyes shining. "I'm on the second floor so we can take the stairs. C'mon."

I hate myself for staring at her ass as I follow her up the stairs. She's wearing a black wool leather coat and tight black pants, along with heavy boots. I'm sure she's trying to look tough, but really, she looks like a little black kitten.

On the second floor, we take a right and we're at a door painted identical to all the others—a wan, industrial gray.

"Kerri and I live here," she says in a hushed voice.

I glance up and down the hall, which is lit with harsh fluorescence. Since I haven't been on a college campus in several decades, I'm curious about something. "Where is everyone? It's so quiet."

Evangeline slides a key into the lock and looks at me quizzically. "Out. It's the weekend. No one stays in. Well, unless they're like tripping on mushrooms or having sex."

As she opens the door, she grins and bites her lip. We enter into her room, and my eyes immediately adjust to the semi-darkness. There appears to be a window, and moonlight is pouring in, a liquid silver that makes Evangeline look maddeningly beautiful.

Maybe it's that moon. Or maybe it's my rage about what her family has done to my people. Or perhaps it's the visceral emotion I feel for her, a shameful, angry, needy lust.

As soon as the door shuts behind us and before she has a chance to turn on a light, I take her by the shoulders and swiftly pin her to the door so I can assault her with my mouth.

What I want is to sink my teeth into her neck, but for the moment, I settle on a punishing, hard kiss.

----

AUTHOR'S NOTE: Odds that he will turn her into a vampire tonight?

----

# Home and Healing and Heaven

**M**atteo moves so quickly that I don't have time to take a breath.

The full weight of his body is hard and heavy against my much smaller frame, pressing me into the door, practically erasing the fact that I exist. His big hand spans my jaw, my chin fitting perfectly into the curve between his index finger and thumb.

I gasp when he yanks my head to one side, his lips against my neck. He moans, and I can feel the vibration of the noise in his body. My hands go into his thick, black hair and I tug, hard. That seems to inspire him even more.

For the first time in my life, I'm afraid. Although this is the moment I've been waiting for, I never considered the fear factor. Never anticipated that this whole turning into a vampire process would be brutal and violent. Silly, stupid me.

When his warm breath hits my neck, a shiver spirals through my body. It's not a shudder of fear, though. It's arousal, stark and heady. When he grips my hair, when he kisses my ear, when he sighs like that, almost like he's pissed—he dominates me a fraction more.

Why am I reacting like this to him? Just a second ago, I was terrified. Am still terrified. A dizzy sensation overtakes me, and I feel like I'm melting into him, pouring my body and soul into every one of his molecules.

Silly. Stupid. Idiot. He shrugs off his jacket, then strips me of my coat, allowing both to crumple onto the floor. I'm only wearing a black tank top underneath, because I thought I'd be hot at the club. Matteo runs his hands down my bare arms, sucking in a breath.

Any moment, he'll rip into my flesh. He'll suck my—

"Why the fuck do you have to be so beautiful, Evangeline?" His hoarse voice shatters my thoughts. The tone is almost desperate, which is shocking. Is he not as commanding as I thought? Or is he equally enthralled by... whatever's going on between us?

He presses a soft kiss to my neck, then trails his lips and nose over my skin while tightening his grip on my chin.

"What?" I gasp.

"I said," he pauses near my ear, "Why the fuck do you have to be so beautiful? You're making this quite difficult for me, amore."

He straightens so we're face to face, and I rake in an inhale when I see his glowing scarlet eyes. He's the real deal, an actual vampire. "What are you talking about? What's difficult?"

"Shh," he hisses, hoisting me into his arms.

What the hell? Part of me wants to yell, wants to demand to know what, exactly, is so difficult for him. The way I figure it, he's a male vampire. He either wants to fuck me or feed from me. I'm fully on board with either, but I also want everything to be nice and simple.

I get the impression that Matteo Moretti isn't a simple man. Nor is he nice.

And although I'm a virgin, I'm not entirely inexperienced with guys. I've done everything but actual intercourse with lots of them, because I've been waiting for the right person.

And I've found him tonight...

Matteo takes a couple of steps into the room. Since he doesn't bang his leg on Kerri's wastebasket like I do every day, I can only assume that he has hyper-sensitive vision. One more step, and when he's about to lay me down, I yelp.

"Uh, this is Kerri's bed," I say with a little laugh, breaking the weird vibe in the room after his strange statement. "My bed's over there. She's pretty open minded and all, but wouldn't appreciate us fooling around in her spot."

He grunts something unintelligible—possibly in Italian, or merely a sound of exasperation—and swings around to walk across the room to the only other bed. It's not like it's that big of a space for two people, and for a second, I'm embarrassed to be doing this here with a man who's god knows how old, and has probably slept in some of the world's finer hotels.

Has he noticed Kerri's collage of Robert Smith from the Cure that's hanging on the wall near her bed? Or my Robert Mapplethorpe poster of Patti Smith? Something tells me Matteo has clinically accounted for and categorized every detail here.

Or maybe not. Maybe I've managed to meet an average vampire who stays at Motel Six and eats at Denny's. Doubtful, though. Not if his Italian-accented English and his slightly formal speech is any indication.

Plus, from what I've read in old books, Italian vampires are the wealthiest of all, the most privileged. Also the most difficult and deadly. Not that it matters right now; it's not like I want to be anywhere but this room.

I figure he'll toss me down and immediately climb on top of me, ready to do whatever he pleases. That's what other guys have done. Instead, he lays me gently on the bed atop my black comforter and pillows. He kneels on the bed and starts to undo his watch from his left wrist. His movements are languid and methodical, all the while watching me with those glowing red eyes.

They're a little unsettling, to be honest.

While he unbuckles his watch that glints in the moonlight, I reach behind me on the shelf built into my wooden headboard. That's where my Sony Dream Machine, a little white digital clock radio, sits. I know the exact button to press, and when I do, my favorite radio station comes on, playing one of my favorite songs. The beat matches perfectly with my heart, and the female singer's voice captures the moment in a sublime, sensual way.

"Well, that's serendipity," I murmur.

"What is?" He sets the watch next to the clock, then lowers himself atop me.

"This song. I love it."

He dips his head to kiss me slow, pressing his hips into mine. He's taut and hard everywhere. The funny thing is, when he's kissing me like this, or like in the club, it's perfect. It feels like... finally. The moment is here. His lips feel like home and healing and heaven on earth.

We kiss the hell out of each other for the entirety of the song, and I lose myself in the moment because it's so, so, so perfect.

Then he thrusts slowly against me, and the movement is so dirty that I can feel my skin practically light on fire. I'm beginning to doubt if I'm going to even survive this night.

"Never heard it. What's it called? I like the beat."

How odd, that he's never heard one of the biggest songs of this decade. Or maybe not? How in touch with pop culture are European vampires, anyway? I run my fingers over his chest, which is covered by a plain black T-shirt. The full effect of his scent is everywhere, and I feel like pausing to bathe in its spicy decadence.

I shut my eyes for a second. "Running Up that Hill by Kate Bush."

A cool sensation overtakes me and my eyes snap open. He's sitting up, pulling his black-T-shirt over his head, the moonlight pouring into the room highlighting a sculpted chest and muscular abs. I want to touch him everywhere. Will he let me?

Matteo reaches for the hem of my tank top and begins to tug it up, over my belly and my breasts. The feel of his fingers on my bare skin sends goosebumps racing up my arms and a squirmy feeling in my stomach. Since I'm small up top, I'm not wearing a bra, which is a little embarrassing—at least until he growls appreciatively when he takes in my breasts.

His hands slide up my body and his thumbs rake roughly over my nipples, which are practically aching because they're so taut. It's if they're seeking his hands, and I arch my back.

"You're going to fucking kill me with your beauty, Evangeline." That's the last thing he says before he starts consuming me with his kisses.

———

AUTHOR'S NOTE: Uh-oh.

———

# Even Angels Fall

Matteo eases onto his shoulder, so he's at my side on the bed. And then somehow, he's pulled me on top of him, quicker than a blink. My heart's beating so fast it's like a wild animal caged by my ribs, rattling my bones to escape.

"Sit up so I can see you, Evangeline."

I comply, and his hands cup my breasts, the silver moonlight splashing on my bare flesh. I'm straddling him, and I wonder if he can feel me shaking. "How can you see me if it's dark?" I murmur as I scoop my hair up, trying desperately to get air on the fever-hot skin of my neck.

"I happen to have excellent eyesight." His statement is benign but the way he says it, all low and rough, makes it sound like the filthiest sentence in the world. He's pinching my nipples between his thumb and forefinger, hard enough to make me wet. Hard enough to make me squirm. Hard enough to want him even more.

Of course he can see perfectly in the dark. He's a vampire. I also have pretty good sight, but probably not like he does.

I roll my hips, so I grind against the hardness in his pants. He lets out another low, menacing growl, only this time, it seems like it's not coming from a person, but a… thing.

He reaches up and puts his hand around the back of my neck, pulling me down toward him, against his mouth. His kisses are downright intoxicating. They're punctuated with little moments of intensity, like when he stops and presses his forehead into mine, his eyes closed, as if he's trying to gather his strength. He does this while holding my hip with one hand, moving my body against his in the most delicious, dirty way.

For a creature that's not human, he's surprisingly passionate. It's a mind-fuck, knowing that he doesn't harbor the same emotions as a human, and yet I almost feel the need and desire pouring from him. Maybe I'm just projecting my own feelings?

I whimper at the sudden realization that he's not like me, not exactly, well, not even a little. He's not even similar Kerri, who's learned to feed by stealing donations from the blood bank where she works. She claims she's become more evolved over the years, that female vampires have more self-control. I guess I'll find out soon enough if that's true.

Matteo kills people by drinking their blood, and that's what's going to happen to me tonight. A flash of indecision washes over me. Should I want this? Do I want this? My life is pretty wonderful right now. I'll relinquish my human existence for what, exactly?

Immortality?

Power?

The ability to help others for eternity?

Yes this is what I want, to fulfill not only my desire, but reverse a horrific legacy started by my ancestors.

But I won't know how I'll feel as a vampire until it happens, and it's too late to turn back now...

"I liked being under you better," I purr, the ache in me surging. If only he'd strip me naked, touch me everywhere, bewitch my body with his touch.

"You did, did you? Hmm. I like you either way, but when you're sitting on me, it's more difficult for me to give in—"

His words are cut off by the door flinging open, and the overhead light blazing above us. Kerri's suddenly standing in the middle of the room.

"Oh my god," I yelp as I stop dry humping Matteo. I lunge for a pillow to cover my chest. My bulging eyes probably are ringed with messy black eyeliner. "I didn't think you'd be back so soon."

Matteo, sits up slowly. He's shirtless and there's a light pink flush on his pale cheeks. I notice the red of his eyes fading back into bright blue, and he shields his gaze from the light. Then he takes a long, deep breath.

"Oh, shit." Kerri winces, baring her fangs. "You didn't put the sign on the door."

My head falls forward so my face is buried in the pillow. "Sorry."

"The sign?" Matteo asks, raking his fingers through his black hair.

Kerri removes the tack from the laminated picture on the wall next to the door. "We made an agreement that if we're hooking up with someone and we don't want to be interrupted, we put this on the door."

She flashes the eight-by-ten of Johnny Cash flipping a photographer his middle finger.

"But if we're just hanging out but want a little privacy," she flips it over and shows him a picture of Adam Ant beckoning with his index finger, "We put this up. It means, knock first."

Matteo squints at her, then at me, then clears his throat. I want to die from embarrassment.

Kerri sets the photo down on a pile of books. "I'll go grab a Coke in the lounge and let you two finish up. Carry on."

She closes the door before I can ask her to turn out the harsh light.

"I'm... I'm sorry," I whisper.

He turns, his blue eyes blazing. "Don't apologize. You didn't know she'd be coming back."

In the stark light, it becomes obvious that he's much older. Not in a creepy way, because he still looks as though he's about twenty-five. But in a this guy's got his shit together, and I'm sitting here topless in my dorm room with posters on the walls and a pile of dirty laundry in the corner.

There are no tangible clues of his maturity, but a vibe I'm getting from the way he sits, the way he carries himself. Younger, eager guys would pounce on me the moment Kerri left. He's slowly picking up his shirt off the floor and I watch, rapt, at how he's both graceful and primal all at once.

I often find beauty where others don't, and my choice of men is no exception.

"I probably should get going." His voice is quiet, haughty.

Oof. The earlier sensual, hyper-sexual mood is shattered, and the disappointment is palpable in my chest, which feels heavy. "Yeah, okay, sure."

I try to play it off like this is nothing, that I make out with strange guys from clubs all the time. The radio's still playing, and an upbeat song by Erasure sounds tinny and stupid. I hit the button, smacking the song off. Somehow the silence is worse.

"Can you hand me my shirt, please?" I ask.

He walks across the room to pick it up, and I avoid his gaze when he's headed back to me. He kneels on the bed next to me and tilts my head up while sliding the pillow away.

"Come here."

I shiver from the cool air on my chest as he gathers my tank and slides it over my head, then helps me put my arms through the holes. When he gently takes my face in his hands and kisses me softly, I moan and liquefy under his touch.

"I wish..." I stop myself, about to say, I wish you didn't have to leave. But that sounds too needy, and no guy likes a needy girl.

"I wish, too," he whispers against my lips, then slides off the bed into a standing position.

Crap.

I reach for a sweater tangled in the comforter at the foot of my bed and slowly put it on and climb to my feet.

He shrugs on his leather jacket, leaning toward the cork bulletin board where I've tacked photos and reminders of class deadlines.

"Is this your family?" His finger hovers over a photo, and I stand close, hoping he'll put his arm around me. He doesn't.

"Yeah, that's Mom, Dad, my brother John, and me, taken one year at Disney in Florida."

Matteo leans closer, as if he wants a better look at the four of us standing near Cinderella's castle. A small, almost imperceptible frown crosses his brow as he studies the photo. Weird.

"Hey, I can walk you out, I have to sign you out of the book downstairs." I tug at the sleeve of his jacket.

He doesn't answer, and for some reason, his silence sends an ominous chill through me.

————

AUTHOR'S NOTE: Is Matteo too hot and cold?

————

# Lovely and Broken

John Ransom's smirk taunts me from the cheery family photo.

Tall, thin, sandy-haired; he looks nothing like his gorgeous sister, who is standing so close to me that I can feel the warmth of her body on my cool skin. I long to grab her and kiss that mouth of hers again, but the anger inside me is rising. There's no telling what I'd do to her in this state, so I need to leave. And the interruption by her roommate was unfortunate.

"Matteo? You don't have to go. We can just hang out, or sit in the lounge, or—"

I interrupt Evangeline, probably in a voice too abrupt, too harsh. But I don't care, now that I've seen all I need. "No, I should return home."

She blinks a few times and nods. I follow her out the door, through the hall, and down the stairs. We approach a group of drunk, giggling girls in the lobby who fall silent when they see us. Not only do I glower at them, but Evangeline does, as well.

The guy at the desk spots her and his face lights up, which makes my blood boil even more.

"I'm signing him out," she says as she gestures to me before making in the book with a pen.

"Evan, do you and Kerri want to come to my room later to watch MTV? That new Billy Idol video is out." the kid says.

Evan? Is that her nickname? It's both endearing and too rough for her. I scowl, thinking that Evangeline is such a delicate, lovely name. No, I'd never call her Evan. Not in a million years.

She looks to me, then at him, twirling a finger around a lock of her red hair. "No, uh, I'm kinda tired. Thanks, though."

The kid's expression crumples as if his Christmas has been stolen. Too fucking bad. A little surge of triumph runs through me, which is absurd.

She sweeps past me and opens the door, allowing a gust of frigid air inside that bites my face. It's like a slap, it's so bracing. A strike that jolts me out of my musings over the lovely Evangeline.

I'm about to tell her that she doesn't need to walk me outside, but she's on the sidewalk before I can finish. Obviously she wants some dramatic goodbye, a passionate kiss. I have mixed feelings about this, and rake in an inhale of cold air.

I walk outdoors, stuffing my hands into my pockets. Although I can feel cold, it doesn't bother me. I find it more invigorating than anything, and would prefer to be out here in just a long-sleeved shirt. But centuries of mirroring humans and a faint memory of when I was alive means pretending that I'm chilly so people don't ask questions.

There's no one in front of the dorm other than us, and we stand face-to-face.

"You said you were going home. Did you mean Italy?" she asks.

"No. I meant the place I'm staying. I'm in Boston for a little while longer."

She nods, a little smile tugging at the corners of that sinful mouth of hers. "Well. It was, ah, interesting. Tonight, I mean."

"That's one way to put it."

As angry as I am, as much as I loathe her family, as much as I'm suspicious of her very existence, I can't help but cup her face in my hands. There's something about this girl, something I desire—even though I'm simultaneously pissed at myself for my carnal thoughts.

Still. I need her in order to get to her brother. I stroke her soft cheeks with my thumbs. "This isn't a goodbye, you know."

She raises her eyebrows. "It isn't?"

"No. I'll be in touch. I'd like to get together again while I'm here. If you'd like to."

She nods, and I lean in for a slow, sensual kiss. Yeah, I want her, in more than a few ways. The little breathy moan that escapes her mouth is so fucking satisfying. But I'm not doing this to please her. Quite the opposite. I ease away from her and remove my hands from her face.

"Go inside. It's cold."

"Do you want the dorm payphone number?" She asks this in a halting cadence, like she's not sure if she should broach such a topic.

I shake my head. "I know where you live." And where every one of her classes are held, and the address of her childhood home. The only thing I don't know is the whereabouts of her murderous brother.

But that's where you'll come in, lovely Evangeline.

She grins. "Okay. You can always leave a note at the desk if I'm not here. See you around."

My gaze follows her as she goes back into the building, and I can't help but notice that she doesn't even pause to chat with the guy behind the desk.

\* \* \*

Instead of taking a cab, I walk the mile or so to the flat on Beacon Hill, hoping to clear my mind. My thoughts are a tangle of confusion as I make my way up Marlboro Street.

It's around one in the morning, and a soothing calm settles over me, as it always does in the hushed darkness. This is my preferred time, when humans are just settling into sleep. For me, there are still many productive hours in this day.

As I stalk up this street lined with stately brownstones and cherry trees on the verge of blossoming, I think about Evangeline. Her scent clings to my skin, and with each inhale I feel a mixture of rage and lust. My steps grow light and soundless against the concrete sidewalk, and in the black of night, I'm sure I resemble a shadow flitting through the night.

How much does Evangeline know about her brother John? Does she understand that he's trying to resurrect their ancestor's plot to infect vampires with a deadly virus? Is she in on that plan? The fact that she's studying to become a doctor is highly suspicious.

It's plausible that she's aligned with John, but doesn't entirely make sense, either. As a half-human, half-vampire, she should have an inkling that I'm a full-blooded creature. Most half-bloods don't want anything to do with my kind. And yet, she wasn't afraid of me, not even a little. She seemed to want everything I did, and Lord knows I wanted so much from her.

Would've taken it, too, if her cock-blocking roommate hadn't come in. That girl's another problem, I can tell.

Logic tells me that I should proceed with pursuing Evangeline's brother and forget about her. Don't involve her in my vendetta, since she could easily become a casualty. Simply because her ancestor's evil virus killed my best friend hundreds of years ago, doesn't mean she's guilty—or that she's on board with her brother's plans to unleash the virus once again to finish the rest of us off.

But luring her brother out of whatever hole he's hiding in would be so much easier if she were my bait. After spending tonight with her, after hearing her sweet, girlish voice, looking into those guileless green eyes, feasting on that velvet-soft skin... I would find it difficult to believe that her brother would ignore her if she was in peril.

And if I'm being honest with myself—which I'm capable of doing, hell, I've spent enough time navel-gazing over the decades—I have ulterior, entirely personal motives. I want to see Evangeline again, for purely physical reasons.

Yes, I want to fuck her.

It's a crude impulse, to be sure. I'm fairly certain I can do it without turning her into a living dead girl. That threat needs to come later, when I'm trying to lure her vampire-hating brother to me. But before that, I want to feast on her flesh in a different way, sate my desire that's gone unquenched for far too long. Don't I deserve as much for this interminable hell, this infernal assignment?

The memory of Evangeline's mouth on mine is fresh, a sweet-hot lingering sting, bracing like the cold wind. There's also a taste of the forbidden, of course, and a twinge of guilt.

Because hunters like me have but a few rules in The Council, and one is to never get involved with a half-breed like Evangeline. Not under any circumstances, but especially under these circumstances. My elders in The Council would want me to kill her without question or mercy, given her heritage.

By merely kissing her, I've already broken several rules of my mission.

And you know what? I've always been a rule breaker, ever since I was turned. Damiano and I both were this way, and I still am. It's why The Council sought me out for this job, to find John and slay him so he doesn't carry out his evil plans.

What The Council doesn't know is that I don't give a fuck about their rules, at least when it comes to Evangeline. I'll get what I want from her and kill her brother, and perhaps finally, Damiano's death will be avenged.

———

AUTHOR'S NOTE: What do you think so far? I'm really looking for feedback since this is my first paranormal romance!

# Dangerous

I find Kerri in the dormitory lounge on the second floor, down the hall from our room. In the semidarkness, she's drinking a Diet Coke, smoking a clove cigarette, and staring out the window.

Not many people in the dorm use the lounge, especially on weekend nights. Most of us go out, either to clubs or parties, or stay in our rooms and drink. The lounge is rarely an option, which is probably why it's turned into Kerri's unofficial domain.

The lounge is charmless, just an empty room with a couple of tired sofas and a few chairs. There are no curtains, no games, no books, no TV, no pay phone When I first moved in, I thought it was a storage area.

But Kerri loves it here, especially at night. It's where she comes to think and smoke.

"Hey," I say softly, not wanting to startle her. She's stretched out on one of the sofas and the entire room smells sweet and spicy, the scent of her cigarettes mixed with her Calvin Klein Obsession perfume.

She shifts so she's sitting up, and I plop next to her on the scratchy
blue sofa. The normally harsh overhead lights aren't on, but it's not
totally dark, since the blazing red-white illuminating triangle on the
CITGO sign in Kenmore Square pours into the room. Kerri basks in
the glow of the sign like a cat with a sunbeam. One time I asked her
if the strong glow didn't hurt her sensitive vampire eyes and she just
laughed and laughed.

"Oh, Evan." She'd let out a giggle, and I could tell from her tone
that I amused her.

Tonight I won't ask any stupid questions, but still brace myself for
a reprimand. I'd seen the flash in her eyes when she burst into the
room and gazed upon the beautiful, shirtless Matteo. It was a look
I'd never seen on Kerri's face before. Was it one of recognition? Envy?
Or something else? I'm certain she'll let me know, because Kerri never
censors herself.

I rest my head on her shoulder, and the thought flashes through my
mind that in many ways, Kerri is the mom I always wanted — despite
the fact that she looks my age. She's older than my own mother,
technically. Well, in vampire years she's older, because she was born
before Mom. But Mom started aging after she had me, so now she's
older than Kerri. Sometimes vampire math is tiring.

"Are you going to lecture me?" I ask.

"It depends."

"On what?"

"How far did you go with him?" She takes a drag and blows out a
cloud of clove-scented smoke that surrounds us like fog.

"Just kissing. A little bit more."

"Okay, not as bad as I thought."

"He doesn't seem like a bad person." I realize I sound petulant, which doesn't sit well. My words are also patently wrong. Matteo might not be evil, but he's definitely not good, either. Even I know this. "I mean, he's hella sexy."

"He's dangerous." Her words hang in the air, mingling with the smoke.

I shift back so I can study her profile, trying to regulate my heart-beat. She's right, of course, but it's not what I want to hear.. "Why do you think so? Do you know him?"

She shakes her head. "Doesn't look familiar. But I've been in the States for a long time. What's his name?"

"Matteo. Said he's from Italy. Has the accent and everything." A truly alluring accent, one that sends pleasurable shivers up my spine just remembering its melodic cadence.

She twists her head to stare at me, and for a second, I spot the same red glimmer in her eyes that I'd seen in his earlier in the evening. "Italy?"

I hum a yes.

"I like this even less now," she mutters, almost to herself.

"Why? And are you sure he's a..."

"I'm certain he's a vampire. Surely you noticed that he was, as well. You're perceptive. You have the ability."

"Yeah, I thought he was. Because of his eyes. They're like yours only..." I allow my voice to trail off, thinking of the intense fire in those eyes of his, and how quickly they'd changed from red to blue, far quicker than I'd ever seen Kerri's shift.

"Only what?"

"Redder, more intense."

"That's because he wants you. Bad. I'm a little shocked that he was able to refrain from feeding from you, but him being from Italy explains a lot." She sighs.

"What does it explain?" My voice rises an octave, revealing my frustration. Sometimes Kerri was too cryptic.

"Generally, but not always, Italian vampires are enforcers. They punish those that want to harm the vampire clan. Most of them travel the world to seek revenge on another vampire, or a human, or another supernatural being that's gotten on the wrong side of the clan. They're dangerous as hell. They're also legends, because they have an enormous amount of self-control."

My breath catches in my throat. This is new information to me. All the research I'd done never mentioned this, and neither had Kerri in the years I'd known her.

"You never told me about these Italians."

"Why would I? Had no reason to. It's not like it ever came up in conversation."

"Well, I dunno about that." Now it was my turn to grumble. I'd grilled her about vampire lore in our first year as roommates. That was four years ago. When she discovered who I was—and who my ancestors had been—she'd helped me close some knowledge gaps. But clearly, she hadn't told me all she knew.

"Although the existence of these vampires, and the group they follow, isn't exactly secret. But it's also not common knowledge. Most vampires like myself have no contact with them. It's like the mafia in the human world. Do you know a mafioso?"

"No," I admit.

She finishes her cigarette and stubs it out in the little tin ashtray stolen from McDonalds that balances on the sofa arm. "Exactly. So why would I ever tell you about them? In all my years, I haven't spent much time thinking about the Italian vampires. I'm aware of their existence, like the way I'm aware of Ronald Reagan or something."

I sneer at the sound of Reagan's name. As much as I hate politics in general, I think I hate the Reagans more, with their stupid Just Say No bullshit.

"You're not going to see Matteo again, are you?" Kerri asks.

"Dunno. He said he wanted to hang out again. Take me to dinner."

Kerri lets out a strangled groan. "Please don't. I'm begging. I've literally never asked you for anything before, but I'm asking you now. Don't see him again. Pretend to be busy. Let me answer your calls. Did he give you his number?"

"No."

"Good. Did you give him the dorm pay phone number?"

"No, he just said he knew where I lived and that he'd see me soon." Come to think of it, that seems more nebulous now than it did a half hour ago. "Maybe he's not interested in seeing me again."

"Oh Jesus."

"What?"

"Do I have to spell it out?" She springs to her feet and she's a silhouette against the red and white neon sign out the window.

"Apparently. And why are you getting so pissed?" Now I'm annoyed, too.

"Because you want something and that particular thing isn't worth the importance you're placing on it."

"I'm an adult. I know what I want. And if Matteo gets me closer to my dream, then great. I don't see why you have a problem with me being... like you."

She paces against the window. "I don't have a problem with you becoming like me. Don't you think I want a friend for eternity? Do you know how hard it is to make friends when you're like me? Jesus. I spent all of the late 1800s alone."

"But you said you had a blast in the Roaring Twenties with Louis Armstrong."

An exasperated snort came out of her mouth. "Whatever. Listen. It's just not all that fun being undead. And you've got the whole thing about the mate looming over your head. That sucks most of all."

"And you don't think human women have something similar with boyfriends and husbands? Please. Ever since I was little, my Mom said I'd eventually meet a nice man, hopefully a doctor, and settle down with kids. It sounds boring and tedious. I don't want a husband or a mate. I just want what I want, and what I want is eternal life so I can spend the next ten or twenty or hundred decades finding a cure for various viruses that plague vampires. I'd think you'd want me to achieve my goals."

A thought crossed my mind that perhaps Kerri didn't believe in me. That she didn't think I was smart enough to become a top researcher that helped vampires. Maybe she thought I was ditzy, or unmotivated, or worse, not serious.

Kerri leans against the window, a perfect silhouette against the bright sign outdoors. "I think your goals are important, and noble. I also think they can be achieved in one lifetime. You've already got so much going for you, in terms of intellect, health, strength. You have the best of both worlds, and you'll live longer than most humans, at least until a hundred. That should be more than enough time to find a cure—"

"I want more time than that. I'm greedy."

"Are you prepared to constantly search for your mate? Because that's what life ends up being after several decades. You begin to search because you're just so sick of your existence in limbo, and you figure that mating and turning back into a human is far better than this." She waves her hand in the air.

"I'll deal with that when the time comes. There's plenty to occupy me in the meantime." Personally, I can't imagine having Kerri's attitude, wanting to find a mate so one could become mortal.

"And what about your parents? Aren't they going to be angry? Have you really, seriously, considered the fallout of that?"

I'm about to reply with something flippant, like "screw my parents," because that was how I feel most of the time. They've been emotionally unavailable at best for the majority of my life. But really, my parents don't factor in to my desires.

"It's my life, not theirs."

She heaves another sigh. "All right. I'm not going to worry about it tonight. Hopefully in the clear light of day you'll reconsider."

No chance of that, I thought as I recalled how Matteo had gripped my chin with enough force to make me notice his strength. Something in that one gesture inspired a tightness inside my body, a feeling of coiled anticipation, and I hoped to have the chance to experience it again.

All I wanted now was to climb into bed and think about that gesture, feel that coiling, over and over again. It wasn't the real thing, but it would suffice.

"I'm headed to sleep, I think." I tried to keep my tone soft and conciliatory, because after all, Kerri was my best friend and I didn't want to end the night on a bad note.

"Good plan." She threads her arm through the crook of my elbow and we walk out together. My shoulders relax with relief. We're parading down the hall, with her humming a Blondie tune. I'm about to belt out one of the lines in the song when we round the corner and almost run smack into the RA.

She's wearing a lumberjack, red-and-black plaid onesie, and Kerri lets out a giggle.

"I've been looking for you," the RA says.

We stop, but don't unlink arms. The RA eyes us. She's always so judgmental. Kerri taps her black, boot-covered foot.

"There's someone downstairs for you, Lana."

I frown. It's past midnight. No one ever visits me. "For me? Who?"

The RA snorts. "I dunno. He refused to leave his name. He looks like one of your friends, though."

My lips part in a silent gasp. Matteo? Why would he come back here?

"What's that supposed to mean?" Kerri asks in a haughty tone. "One of your friends?"

The RA pushes past us. "You know. Goth or punk or whatever. One of your type of freaks."

"At least we're well-dressed and interesting, unlike your boring ass," Kerri mutters. "C'mon, Lana let's see what the Italian loverboy wants."

She tugs my arm, but I'm rooted to the floor. Kerri's words echo in my brain, the ones about Matteo being an enforcer. What did that mean, exactly?

Something tells me that if Matteo's downstairs, it's going to be mortifyingly embarrassing, or possibly worse.

EDITOR'S NOTE: How are you feeling about this story so far? Do you like Evan and her motivation to be a vampire?

———

# Blood Sucking Vermin

Kerri and I take a few steps down the hall, and she pushes open the door to the stairs leading to the first floor.

As she's about to bound down, I speak up. "Uh, I'll go by myself. I'll meet you back in the room."

"Nope. I'm coming with you. This is a highly unusual situation." Her voice echoes in the old stairwell that smells like sneakers. The temperature in here is a good ten degrees cooler than it is in the main part of the building, and I wrap my arms around my midsection.

There's no use arguing with her, so I follow. Kerri has what my mother would call a "strong personality," and the times I've tried to talk her in—or out—of something, I've never been successful. And, she's correct. It is a highly unusual situation.

My mind spins as I wonder why Matteo would've returned. Did he leave something in his room? His watch, maybe? I scan my brain. I remember him taking it off, the way the moonlight glanced off his sharp cheekbone. But I don't recall him putting it back on.

That must be it. The watch. Then again, I was in a fog in those moments after Kerri walked in on us. It was as if he'd wiped my mind blank with his kisses.

Kerri yanks open the door to the lobby and holds it open for me. I try to project as much confidence as she possesses on a normal day, and strut through.

I round the corner, making eye contact with the desk person—it's not my friend Alex, it's someone new, since there's been a shift change—and glance around. There's no one in the lobby, at least not this part of it. Usually visitors linger by the desk in one of the two tired chairs that match the sofa in the lounge upstairs. The rest of the place is empty, the building's once-grand mosaic tile floor scuffed and faded.

"Hey, I'm Evangeline Ransom. My RA said someone was here for me." I pause, then add helpfully, "A guy."

The desk person, a girl younger than me who looks baby-faced and bored, puts down her Spin Magazine and nods. "Oh. Yeah, he's in the bathroom. Said he'd be right out."

I thank her and Kerri and I shuffle to the middle of the lounge.

My gaze meets Kerri's. For some reason, the idea of a powerful Italian vampire taking a leak in an ancient college dorm in Boston's Back Bay strikes me as funny. The downstairs bathrooms are notoriously filthy. Legendarily so, on weekends, due to all the partiers.

The side of my mouth quirks up.

"Even vampires need to piss," Kerri whispers, and I dissolve in a fit of giggles. Probably I'm exhausted, but the entire situation makes my body shake with laughter. I try to calm myself but Kerri crosses her eyes and sticks out her tongue and that just makes me laugh harder.

I need to get ahold of myself. The last thing I want is Matteo walking out from the men's room, thinking Kerri and I are laughing at him. I wander off to stare at a bulletin board of announcements. It takes reading a flyer for a movie night five times to calm down. Do I want to see St. Elmo's Fire? Eh. Looks boring.

I hear a door swing open, and I want desperately to whirl around to greet Matteo. But that's probably the wrong thing to do, so I keep staring at the flyer.

Kerri clears her throat and I turn to glance at her. The expression on her face is no longer silly, it's incredulous.

"Wha—" I'm about to squawk out the word when my eyes are drawn like magnets to the third person in the room.

It's not Matteo, not even close.

It's my brother, John.

With a yelp, I leap across the room and wrap my arms around him. I haven't seen him in so long that it's almost like I want to make sure it's really him, and not a mirage.

"Oof." He laughs and hugs me back, just as hard.

"Where have you been? When did you get back? As usual, Mom and Dad didn't say anything. Did you see them? Or did you just fly in? How was Europe? I missed you, oh my God—"

"Whoa, whoa, whoa, Evan. One question at a time."

I pull back to look at John. He's sturdier than when I last saw him, as if he's gone to the gym or eaten more. The last time I saw him—in that family photo taken at Disney, the one Matteo was staring at in my room—he was a skinny kid with peach fuzz on his jaw. Now he's broad-shouldered, with a sprinkling of dark golden stubble on his jaw. His hair's still the same, though, unruly and messy, giving him an I-don't-give-a-shit aura. Which always upset Mom.

His green eyes, which are the same color as mine, shift from me to Kerri. In a flash, I see his gaze harden, then relax. It's an imperceptible thing, and y muscles involuntarily tense.

"This is my roommate Kerri." I gesture to her. "Kerri, this is my brother John. You know, the one I'm always talking about, the one in the pictures."

Kerri nods and looks him up and down, probably sizing him up as a potential hookup. She's a bit predatory when it comes to men, and the idea that she'd do anything with my brother makes me feel uncomfortable. And a little grossed out, to be honest.

My friends in high school always told me that my older brother was hot. I never believed them. But it must be true, if the way Kerri's leering at him is any indication. Yikes.

"Hey." Her tone is practically a purr. I fight to not roll my eyes.

"Hey." My brother's voice is clipped, hard. He must be exhausted.

I take his arm. "Let's go up to our room. We've got wine, and Pop Tarts."

John reaches over and musses my hair, which is already pretty tangled after my romp with Matteo. "My palate has evolved from box wine and Pop-Tarts, Dimples."

I glower at him for using his childhood nickname.

"Dimples?" Kerri asks.

"Shut up," I reply.

"That's what I used to call her. Because, see?" He pretends to wrestle my face in his hands, poking his index finger into my cheek while Kerri snickers. "Under this scary goth façade is a perfect, angelic dimple."

"Whatever," I say crossly. "Let's go upstairs. It's cold in here. We also have a space heater."

"I'm hungry. I want a slice of pizza. I saw a place that looks like it's open all night in Kenmore square. C'mon."

"That place is so gross," I protest. "All of the slices are greasy."

He glances again at Kerri, who's literally licking her lips and staring in the direction of his crotch. John leans into me and says in a low voice, "But just the two of us, okay?"

Kerri, who has the sharpest hearing of anyone I know, sniffs in annoyance. She shrugs off her leather jacket. "Here. Wear this. It's freezing outside. I'm headed to bed, anyway. This night has been shit."

She hands me her jacket, and I slip it on, allowing her pungent perfume and clove smell to envelop me. "Thanks for this. We'll be back pretty soon."

"I trust your brother to keep you safe." She leans toward him, and I can't help but notice her taking a long, deep inhale in the direction of his neck. In addition to her amazing hearing, her sense of smell is like a bloodhound's. One of the many perks of being a vampire, I guess.

"Sure, sure," he says, stepping away from her as if she's got leprosy. Weird.

Kerri clomps away, disappearing behind the door to the stairwell. John looks at me and raises an eyebrow. "Ready?"

Even though it's almost two in the morning and cold as a witch's tit, we make our way outside.

"Seriously, John. It's been so long. Where have you been? I've been worried sick. Every time I ask Mom and Dad, they say they don't want to discuss it. Or you."

"Yeah, I've been pretty much disowned."

"I don't understand. I've never understood." John was four years older than me, so by the time I started college, he'd already graduated. After getting his diploma from Colby College in Maine not far from where we grew up, he took a year off to travel in Europe, and then enrolled in the London School of Economics. Frequent letters and infrequent, expensive long-distance calls had been our only connection for two years.

I'd planned on visiting John this semester, but the weird falling out with our parents had made me hesitate.

Now that he's here, guilt washes over me. Our parents are difficult even during the best of times. John's been on his own, in a foreign city. Why didn't I make more of an effort to call him? I could've used the money from my work study job in the college financial aid office to buy calling cards. Instead, I used my paycheck to buy new Betsey Johnson dresses at that store on Newbury Street.

I'm a terrible sister. But John also hadn't made much of an effort, and his last letter, which came only a few weeks ago, said that he'd found a group of friends in London. I'd worried a little less about him after that. "I'm sorry about Mom and Dad," I say softly.

"I'm not." John's voice is flat and loud. It echoes against the pillars of the highway underpass, the one I walked through earlier that evening with Matteo. I shiver, recalling those hours with him. What would John think of Matteo?

"What happened between you, anyway?"

"I'll tell you when we get inside, out of the cold." He's wearing jeans, black boots, and a black wool coat. Also a black knit cap. Somehow it makes him look quite English and proper. Even his speech has adopted a twinge of British formality, mixing with his Maine accent.

"Okay." We continue in the darkness, the temperature seemingly dropping with each step. "It is freezing out here. Jeez Louise."

"Stop it. You don't need to be nervous around me. I'm your brother."

"Well, of course I'm nervous. I haven't seen you for years, there's some big rift between you, Mom and Dad, and then you show up out of the blue, in March. Why aren't you in school? Surely you haven't graduated. What's going on? And you look different, too. I'm worried about you."

"You're the only one," he says softly. "You've always loved me more than anyone, Evan."

We're about to step from of the shadows of the underpass when I notice a man approaching us. It's one of the punk guys I've seen working at the record store in Kenmore Square. He's got jet-black, spiky hair and is dressed in head-to-toe leather. Handsome, but he's never given me the time of day. Nor Kerri. And god knows she's tried to catch his attention.

I don't think he's a student. He's always aloof, except when you ask him about the latest release from Bauhaus. Only then does he show any emotion.

John moves closer to me, a gesture I assume is one of chivalrous protection. He's always been old fashioned like that, and since he's not a goth or a punk, I figure he's unnerved by the guy coming toward us. I'm obviously not scared, because, well, who would be? He's a skinny, pale punk guy in possession of excellent hair gel and great taste in music.

A sneer forms on my brother's face. John's always been more of a preppy type, and I brace myself for a smarmy comment. I'm sure he also doesn't like my choice of clothing, either. Also this explains his disdain for Kerri.

The spiky hair guy glances our way when he's about two feet from us, and for a fraction of a second, his eyes flash red. A thrill flows through me. Is he a vampire? How did I not know this after all these instances of running into him at the record store? Interesting.

I'm about to nod hello when my brother shoves me aside. I almost fall into a muddy, brown snowbank.

"What are you doing?" I stammer. "J-John?"

"Not tonight, fangs," he yells at the guy.

John's arm is extended, and he's gripping a silver cross that glints in the wan streetlight. A murderous expression clouds his normally placid face. What's gotten into him?

I gasp my brother's name.

"Stay back, Evan. I won't let this blood sucking vermin touch you."

The spiky hair guy stops, sneers, then spits on the ground in between he and my brother. His eyes are fully red now, much like Matteo's were earlier in the evening. Fear showers through my body. Yes, I want to be a vampire.

But not this way. Not out here, and not now, and definitely not with my brother present. Will the spiky hair guy attack us? How can I diffuse this situation?

What a fucking crazy night this has been.

John takes a step toward the guy, saying something in Latin. It's like a bad movie, what he's doing.

I've had enough. "For God's sakes, put that away," I snap at John.

"Listen to her," the guy says in a thick Boston accent. "She's way smarter than you are, buddy. She knows the score."

The guy snorts dismissively and turns. John shoves the cross back into his pocket and I take his arm, dragging him toward the pizza place a few blocks away.

"What the fuck was that, John? Why are you accosting random people? Even if he was a vampire, he's harmless. I see him all the time at the recor—"

John stops and grabs my upper arms. "Do not ever defend a vampire again. Not to me. You need to promise to stay away from him."

"Why? Let me go. What has gotten into you?" Like me, John is a half-vampire, half-human. He'd never been interested in our heritage, not like I had. Or so I thought.

"And your roommate. I need to know everything about her." His voice is a demand.

"What about her?" Now I'm cross, wishing he'd never come. This isn't the John I knew, the goofy kid who slipped me Stephen King paperbacks when I was in middle school.

"You want to know why Mom and Dad disowned me?" He shakes me by the arms.

"Stop, you're hurting me! What does Mom and Dad have to do with why you're flashing a cross at random people on the street?" His fingers dig into my shoulders, sending flash points of pain into my brain. I struggle against his grip, and then still when he violently yanks me toward him.

"Because it's my life's goal to kill as many vampires as possible, and Mom and Dad don't think that's a viable career choice for their first born."

AUTHOR'S NOTE: Eek! A new twist. What are your thoughts on John?

——

# Rage

I inhale a lungful of icy air, and it's as if the cold is seeping into every cell in my lungs.

"You... what?" I ask John.

When he laughs, whatever part of my body managed to stay warm until this point is now frigid and still. His chuckle is downright evil. I've never heard him sound this way.

I exhale and the steam from my breath surrounds the two of us in a gray plume against the night sky.

"C'mon. Let's go get pizza. I'll tell you all about it." He marches off, and I hesitate. He's acting like this is normal, and that's deeply disturbing.

Should I follow? Especially given that my best friend is a vampire—and considering that I want to also be an immortal?

This must be a joke. I'm need to find out what's going on with my brother. I power-walk to catch up with him.

Thank God we're silent during the few short blocks to the pizza place. A crushing feeling of sadness hits me, because at one time,

John and I were thick as thieves. I remember when I was in middle school and he was a high school sophomore, how he'd help me with homework and take me skiing at a small mountain in Maine.

We never even had typical brother-sister fights; Mom always marveled at this. "Somehow I raised perfect children," she'd brag to her friends.

Which is what makes his absence—and this unannounced visit—all the more shocking.

At the Boston House of Pizza, John holds the door open for me. The place is blazing with fluorescent light, jam-packed, too much to handle in my current confused state. It's well past one in the morning and this is the only thing open for food in Kenmore Square at this time of night.

It's flooded with drunk, poufy-haired suburbanites from Narcissus, the club across the street, arrogant punks from Axis, stone headbangers from the Rathskeller, and a smattering of frat boys. It would be a toxic mix given that three-quarters of the crowd is either drunk or high, but somehow, it's controlled chaos. The air is laced with the odor of cheese, sweat, and beer.

"Go snag that table over there." John points to a booth. "I'll grab our slices. You want Dr. Pepper?"

"Yeah, thanks."

I plop down in the booth and rest my head on my folded arms at the table, exhausted. Between Matteo and my brother, this night has definitely taken a turn for the strange. The only thing I'm thankful for is that John didn't arrive while Matteo was in my room...

"Hey, you want company?"

I look up and there's an older guy with blonde, slicked-back hair standing with a soda at the end of the booth. He waggles his eyebrows. This is all I need, some disco-throwback dude who was desperate for a screw.

"As if," I snort. "Gag me with a spoon." I sometimes revert to Valley Girl speak when I'm sarcastic.

"Bitch," he says, and walks off.

Boston can be such a cold, nasty place. The drivers suck, the people are generally surly, and sometimes it seems like no one has a kind word—unless they want to get laid, of course. Normally I love all of this, but tonight, everything's grating on my nerves.

Finally my brother comes over with a pizza box, two paper plates, and two soda cans balanced on top. "Did that dickhead try to talk to you? Because I'll kill him. Just say the word."

"Calm down, Rambo. Let's just eat." I roll my eyes.

We tuck into the pizza and for a second, it's like nothing strange ever happened. But I'm too curious to ignore what happened earlier.

"So what's really going on, John? What's all this about vampires?" I say the word vampire like I've barely heard of them.

"Well, for starters, I dropped out of school in London."

I gape at him while holding the slice in mid-air. "Why?"

"I connected with group of people. Smart, interesting men, who made me realize how important my heritage, well, our heritage, is."

"What? Are you joking?" I set my half-eaten slice down. I'm suddenly not hungry at all, and the pizza's far too greasy. "What kind of group?"

A cult. He must have fallen in with a cult.

"It's this secret society that hunts vampires." He says this casually, as if it's the most normal thing in the world. Like he accepted a job as an investment banker or something.

"What?" I yelp again.

"Shh. Keep it down."

"How can I keep it down? This is insane. I haven't seen you for years and then you show up one night at my dorm and tell me you are a freaking vampire hunter with some weird English group? What the hell?"

He takes a long sip of his drink and shrugs. "Shit happens."

"No. Shit does not just happen. Especially considering our parents were once—"

"I know what they were. And they had the good sense to find each other and become mortal. Most of them don't want to do that, though." His nostrils flare, as if he can't stand talking about the topic without fury.

"So? What's it to you?" I squirm uncomfortably in my seat. John has no idea what I want to do for a living when I get out of medical school.

"Vampires are a scourge against humanity. They're not natural. They're not human, Evan. I know that a lot of people are okay with them existing. That they live alongside normal people in some areas.

But they shouldn't. They're a menace and they must be eradicated. We can't let them steal our way of life."

I rub my temples with the heels of my hands. What do I even say to this? I'm speechless. It's true that some vampires prey upon people. But most are like Kerri; they've learned to manage their condition. The few that kill people? Hell. Humans kill other humans.

John's voice lowers. "I want to carry on the work of our ancestor. The group in London says it's my duty."

"Our ancestor was a crazy man who developed a deadly virus for the purposes of genocide. And, your duty is to get an economics degree since Mom and Dad are paying for your education."

"Not anymore they aren't." He tears off a piece of crust and stuffs it in his mouth. "Anyway, how's school going for you?"

I gape at him. "You're going to drop this bombshell about becoming a vampire hunter or whatever then ask me how school's going? What has gotten into you? You used to be normal. John, you don't seem okay."

A snort escapes his lips. "You used to be normal, too. A few years ago you never looked like that."

"Like what?" I pick a piece of pepperoni off my slice and pop it in my mouth, pretending not to be wounded by his words. Never in his life has he talked to me like this, in this caustic, judgy tone. Maybe he's on drugs. Or this London group is practicing mind control. I need to tread lightly, that's for sure. Don't want to scare him off before I can get more information.

"Like some stupid undead bride. Christ, Evan. You used to be so cute. I guess that's just fashion, but I hate how the whole 'vampire aesthetic' has taken over." He makes little quote marks with his fingers. "Tell me about that roommate of yours. I got a bad vibe from her."

The pepperoni turns to sawdust in my mouth and I swallow hard. "Kerri? She's awesome."

"Hmph."

I watch him wolf down two more slices, trying to figure out what to say. I definitely won't be telling him about my future plans.

"So, um. Where are you staying? Do you want to crash in my dorm room?"

Please say no. Please say no. It kills me to think that way, because I'd love nothing more than to hang out with my brother all weekend. Well, the guy who was my brother. Not this hate-filled, obsessed rage addict.

"My friends have a safe house in Allston. I'm leaving tomorrow."

"For where? And what time?" Part of me is relieved, but a bigger part is devastated. I need more time with him. More time to figure out what's happened, more time to talk some sense into him.

"Can't say. Secret mission. I'd hoped to see you in Maine a couple of weekends ago. But Mom and Dad wouldn't let me." He fiddles with his napkin, folding it into a tight square.

"Wait. You were in Maine?"

He nods and a shadow of sadness crosses his face. It's the first time he's looked anything but arrogant or enraged all night. "I was there the same time you were. But Dad asked me not to come around. He doesn't agree with what I'm doing."

I don't either, I want to say. But don't, because I can't push him away. My mind is a swirl of emotions and exhaustion. I nod. "What time do you leave?"

John's about to answer when we hear shouting at the front of the pizza place. We both turn our attention to the counter. A guy with long, shaggy hair and a leather jacket pushes a bigger guy in a polo shirt. Both have the telltale flush of intoxication. The words "fuck you" are shouted.

"Looks like some drunk frat boy's about to brawl with a headbanger. Let's get outta here."

"Agreed." Thank god John didn't want to step into that mess. That's one way this evening could get worse.

We quickly walk out as seemingly the entire restaurant forms a circle around the two guys to watch.

"I'll walk you back to your dorm," John says.

Again we're silent as we trudge through the cold. I don't know what to say, what to ask. It's as if my brother has become an instant stranger, and I can't comprehend how to absorb any of this. With every person we pass, I pray that they're not a vampire, or different in any way, because I don't know if he's going to explode.

All I know is that he keeps his hands clenched into tight fists the entire walk.

At the entrance to my dorm, I muster a smile. "What time are you leaving tomorrow?"

"Headed out after dark, we have a flight out of Logan."

"Can we get breakfast together?"

He grins and it seems genuine. "Sure. Want me to come by around seven?"

This makes me laugh. "John, it's almost two in the morning. Can we make it more like nine?"

"You've always been a night owl. C'mere."

He pulls me into a hug. "Goddamn, I've missed you, Evan."

A sob claws at my throat. What the hell has happened to him? I need to find out, but not tonight. when I'm rested, when I'm not a ball of confusion. "Missed you to, John-John."

"Okay, so tomorrow at ten. Pick your favorite spot and we'll go there. Anywhere in the city, okay? Somewhere nice, somewhere expensive."

I nod into his neck. My eyes well with water because of the full force of my emotions hit.

"I'm glad you want to see me. I wasn't sure if Mom or Dad had poisoned the well, so to speak," he says, his voice husky.

We break apart and I shake my head, wondering if I should call Mom when I get upstairs. "They didn't say anything."

"Be safe getting to Allston. Take a cab, okay?"

"I will. Oh, and prepare yourself. You look tired as hell tonight, so I didn't say anything. But I want to talk to you about joining me when you graduate. I think my group could really use someone with your talents and mind."

I blink a few times, the frigid air freezes the tears on my lashes. "Um. Ah. Okay," I croak.

"Get some sleep, Dimples." He musses my hair, like he used to when we were kids, then walks away.

When safely inside the dorm, I sob as I haul myself up the stairs.

———

AUTHOR'S NOTE: Hello, reader friends! I hope you are enjoying The Awakening. I need your help with something!

I love connecting with you on Wattpad, but I'd also like to interact outside of Wattpad! If you could please take a couple of minutes to fill out this very short questionnaire about which social media platforms you use and what type of content you'd like to see from me on social media, that would be amazing!

Thank you!

LINK: https://mail.google.com/mail/u/0/#search/Irina/FMfcg zGllVlDmsPhbzKmwksnHxsLFqCQ

# No Control

"Shit. Shit. Shit."

I fling the covers off my bed. It's nine-forty five in the morning, which means I've overslept. My brother will be here in fifteen minutes, and something tells me he won't be cool if I'm late.

While grabbing my pink plastic shower caddy filled with makeup, Aussie shampoo, Noxzema cold cream, Sea Breeze toner and my toothbrush and toothpaste, I notice that Kerri's not in the room. Oh, right, it's Sunday, which means she's working a shift as a lab tech at the blood bank.

She works at odd hours, testing the blood for AIDS and other viruses. Since she's at the lab with only one or two other people, she's able to feed without anyone noticing. Apparently she ducks into a supply closet to drink while transporting the bags of blood from one room to another.

I'd hoped to talk to her about John last night, but she'd been fast asleep when I got back to the room. And then I'd crashed, exhausted from, well, everything.

My head is still jammed with thoughts while I yank my robe off a hanger and head to the shared bathrooms. Next year when I'm in medical school, I'll have a room to myself, with a bathroom. This sharing crap definitely sucks.

Fortunately, there's no one in any of the shower stalls, and I'm in and out in five minutes. Back in my room, I scrape back my hair into a wet ponytail, then peek outside. It looks cold, gray, and unforgiving. There's no way I should go out with wet hair, but the digital clock is ticking toward ten.

"Screw it," I mutter, twisting my damp hair into a bun and slipping on a black hat. It goes with the rest of my outfit: Docs, leggings, a miniskirt, a turtleneck, a sweater, and then finally, my wool coat. All black, of course.

I don't bother with makeup but do wind a scarlet-colored scarf around my neck before I stomp out of the room. I'm not a morning person, something Mom says I need to work on before medical school.

Ugh, I'd hoped to get up early so I could call Mom and ask her about John. Last night seems like a dream, from my frenzied, hot time with Matteo to the random appearance of my brother. I'm not great with change, which is why I've lived in the same dorm for four years. The events of the past twelve hours have left me feeling deeply unsettled, which is why my stomach feels like I'm digesting ground glass as I step into the lobby.

Which is empty.

I peek outside. Sure enough, it's freezing, one of those bright sunny days that draws the breath out of your lungs because it's so ice-cold. There's no one at the front of the building except that girl on the fifth floor who dresses in pajamas all the time. She's smoking a cigarette and nods at me.

"Hey, did you see a tall guy, brown hair?" I ask.

She shakes her head. "I've smoked two cigarettes and haven't seen anyone."

"Thanks," I mumble, and head back in.

I make my way over to the front desk and spot a familiar face. It's Jasinda, a friendly sophomore who lives on three. She sets down her thick textbook and greets me with a kind smile, and I do the same.

"Has anyone come in asking for me? I'm supposed to meet someone."

"Oh, yes!" She shuffles some papers around. "I was called in at three in the morning because the overnight person was sick. So I'm doing a double. Around four a guy came in with a note for you. Here."

She hands me a torn slip of paper and I nearly gasp when I read the message, written in the most formal cursive I've ever read.

Brunch at my place? Come by when you can, I'll be inside all day. 31 Chestnut Street, Beacon Hill — Matteo

"Oh my God," I whisper. An electric current runs through me as I trace his words with my thumb.

"Girl, that man who left that note was fine. A little too pale for my taste, but damn. He took out this wild pen. Like a real fountain pen, and spent what seemed like two minutes writing that note."

My heartbeat thunders in my ears. I look up at Jasinda and stammer several ums and ahhs. "You saw him?"

She shoots me a salacious grin. "I sure did. He came in here with a gust of wind like something out of a movie. Kinda scared the crap out of me, but he was so polite and hot I couldn't help but ogle him a little. If that's your boyfriend, sorry about that."

"Eh. Not my boyfriend," I say slowly. It's too early for all this intrigue. "But no one else came in this morning for me?"

"Nope. It's been real slow. Everyone must've gotten good and drunk last night, because the entire dorm's been pretty quiet."

I mumble a thanks and sink into one of the chairs on the far side of the room. It's not like my brother to be late, but clearly John's changed since the last time I saw him. Also, Boston traffic is pretty hellish so he could've been held up if he's taking a cab.

I stare at Matteo's note, reading and re-reading every word.

Brunch seems so...adult. Old-fashioned, even. No one I know eats brunch; I just scarf down cereal at the cafeteria or if I'm feeling really ambitious, drag Kerri and trek across the city to the vintage South Street Diner, which is like something out of a 1950s movie. She drinks only coffee because she doesn't enjoy most food (she's really into sushi, go figure), but I love their Boston crème pancakes and their hash browns.

Ugh, that's exactly what I want right now. Diner food. My stomach rumbles, and I wish John would get here.

The moments tick past and I continue to analyze the note. If I didn't have plans with my brother, would I go to Matteo's house?

Come by when you can. I'll be inside all day.

Of course he will, because he's a vampire and it's glaringly sunny and bright out. I had been under the impression that vampires couldn't exist in the sun, but Kerri says it's just more uncomfortable, like a raging hangover, for most.

I stand up and begin to pace the obby.

"Girl, no man is worth waiting this long," Jasinda calls out.

I sigh and wander over to her desk. "It's my brother."

"Still. If he can't be on time, he's not worth yours."

The clock on the wall says ten-thirty. The memory of my brother's hard, angry face last night pops into my head. Then his parting words.

I want to talk to you about joining me when you graduate. I think my group could really use someone with your talents and mind.

My gaze goes again to the clock on the wall, then to the handwritten note I'm clutching. My fingers are so sweaty that it's made the ink on the paper bleed in one corner.

"Listen, I'm going around the block to the convenience store for some coffee. I'll be back in ten minutes. If my brother comes, his name is John. You want anything?" I need to work off some of this nervous energy and wake up with a vat of caffeine.

Jasinda shakes her head. "I'll make sure your brother stays put."

Outside, the cold slaps me in the face. I hurry to the store, and fill the biggest Styrofoam cup with black, nasty coffee, then dump a ton of sugar inside.

The whole excursion takes me about ten minutes, and I'm out of breath when I walk back into the dorm, hoping to see my brother waiting for me.

Jasinda shakes her head. "Haven't seen a soul."

I attempt to sip from my cup but the coffee's way too scalding for that.

"Well, if John shows up, tell him I went to brunch."

Jasinda grins. "Should I give him the address on that note? 31 Chestnut Street is an awful nice neighborhood."

I let out a nervous laugh. "Definitely not. Just tell him I'm sorry I missed him."

"You got it."

Feeling a little out of control, I head out and walk to Beacon Street so I can hail a cab. It doesn't take long, and I'm practically shaking as we hurtle down Storrow Drive. What in the hell am I doing? I don't even have a speck of makeup on and probably look like crap.

I tell the cabbie to let me out at Charles and Chestnut so I can walk a few blocks and gather my thoughts. My pace is slow as I make my way down the street lined with cherry trees and historic brick buildings.

Despite all of my layers of clothing, most of my body is chilly, except my hand, which is fused to my warm coffee cup. A lock of damp hair has escaped my hat, and it's now frozen and hard.

What am I going to say to Matteo? What will we walk about? Will we even talk? Does a vampire know how to make brunch? A thousand questions race through my mind as I approach the address.

And then, there it is, on my left. It's a stately brownstone, with black shutters, a black door, and stark white Grecian columns. It's a classic Greek revival home, probably built in the early 1800s (I know this since I took a local architectural history class as an elective two years ago).

Should I keep walking past? Turn around and go to the library? Catch another cab and eat breakfast alone at the diner?

My teeth begin to chatter, either from nerves or the cold. Probably nerves. No, I've come all this way, and Matteo is the one person who can give me what I want. Plus, I feel almost as if the house is pulling me toward it, a flame to my moth. The draw is too strong, and I make up my mind.

I take the eight steps to the door slowly, then am startled when I realize that this hasn't been split into condos; it's an entire house. There's only one buzzer on a brass-plated sign that reads "Damiano Barbieri."

Weird. I wonder who that is. A friend or a relative, I assume. I stab at the button, feeling woozy from the anticipation.

The door swings open. Matteo's standing there, all intense, piercing eyes. He's wearing a loose, white shirt with the top few buttons undone, and black leather pants. His black hair looks freshly washed, and slicked back.

"Hi, I got your note," I blurt. Brilliant opening.

He squints into the sun pouring onto his face, and moves back, opening the door wider. "Evangeline. You came. I'm so pleased. Please, come inside, it's far too cold out there, and I don't want you getting sick."

Against my better judgement, I step inside, into the darkness of the home.

# Stoking a Fire

I didn't think Evangeline would show up, but here she is in my foyer, all wide eyes and rosy cheeks. Heartbreakingly beautiful would be the way I would describe her, but I can't get trapped in the superficial. Not now, not while I'm so close to getting what I need.

"Is this a good time? I'm not interrupting anything, am I? I got your note and..."

Her voice fades when I lean down and kiss her right cheek, then her left, like we do in Italy. Now her cheeks are even rosier, which makes me grin.

"It was an open invitation. I was on my early morning walk and got the idea to invite you over." No need to explain that I was up all night, as usual, because I sleep during the afternoon, if at all. Or that I was wandering the dark streets of Boston for hours in the cold, thinking about her, and her brother.

Now that she's here, I need to pour on the charm. It won't be difficult, because she's so gorgeous. If only she was related to anyone but John Ransom.

"May I take your coat? And what's this?" I tap the plastic top of her coffee cup.

"Oh, I stopped at a convenience store. Can't live without my coffee, you know?" Her laugh is a little too forced and shrill.

This elicits a genuine chuckle from me. "My dear, sweet girl. Give that to me and I'll make you some real coffee."

"Uh, okay." I take the offending cup from her and set it on a side table.

She shrugs out of her heavy wool jacket, and I carefully hang it on a hook in the foyer.

"This is a beautiful house." She rubs her upper arms and that's when I notice a lock of her hair is frozen solid. I reach over and take it in my fingers, wanting to snap it in two.

"Wet hair? Icy hair?"

She nods. "I didn't have time to dry it this morning."

"You're going to get pneumonia. Let's go to the library. I have a fire started."

Normally I'd never light a fire—there's no need, since I'm impervious to cold. But since I suspected, well, hoped, she'd come by, I built a beautiful stack of wood to blaze in the hearth. I have to admit, the aesthetic of the fire in the book-filled room is quite beautiful.

Sensual, even.

"Come." I put my hand on the small of her back and propel her down the hall.

She leans into me and I capture her scent in my nose. I can smell her blood, a rich, heady fragrance. It's so much more evident today, now that she's not awash in perfume and cigarette smoke from that club last night.

"Wow, this home is incredible. They don't make them like this anymore. Greek Revival, right?"

Impressive that such a young woman would even know that term. "Yes. But it's not mine. It's a dear friend's house, and I use it whenever I visit Boston."

"Oh. Damiano?"

"Yes, how did you know?"

I pause at the library door, wanting to shake her for uttering my friend's name out loud. How dare she, with the legacy of her family? With what they did to Damiano?

"It's... it's on the buzzer outside." She blinks, obviously taken aback from my demanding tone.

I force myself to chuckle. "Of course, of course it is."

"Are you here alone? Or are there others?"

"No, it's just me. Well, and a housekeeper who comes twice a week." Another vampire in fact, but I don't tell Evangeline this.

I push open the door to the library and she gasps.

"This is. Wow. Oh wow. I've never seen a private library like this before."

"It is impressive, isn't it?"

She stands in the middle of the room on the scarlet-colored oriental rug, slowly turning in a circle, taking in the floor-to-ceiling mahogany shelves stuffed with books. The library is bathed in the gentle glow of the fire, a warm golden light. The windows are obscured with heavy, red velvet drapes.

"Look at that, a ladder to reach the upper shelves," she murmurs, almost to herself.

At one end of the room is the fireplace, with a large painting over the mantel.

She pauses to stare at it, then takes a step toward the fire. It's the art in the large, gilded frame that's captured her attention, a massive painting depicting a particularly violent scene.

"Whoa. That looks familiar. But no. That can't be." She shakes her head.

"What?" I ask, amused at her befuddlement.

"The painting. I took a European art history class last year, and that looks like Artemisia Genti...Genti... I can't pronounce it."

"Aertemisia Gentileschi," I say in a thick Italian accent.

"Yes. That's it."

"Judith Slaying Holofernes. That's the name of the painting."

"But I thought it was in the Uffizi?" She looks to me, confusion contorting her pretty face.

"Very good. You must have paid attention in class. This is an alternate work done by the artist. A precursor to the one in the Uffizi, if you will."

"No way. That can't be. That's real?"

I laugh, genuinely this time. "You Americans are always so skeptical. My friend Damiano was quite the collector."

"Was? Where is he now? Does he no longer collect art?"

My laughter fades. "Why don't you take your boots off and warm your feet by the fire, while I make you a cappuccino? Feel free to get comfortable, Evangeline."

I squeeze her upper arm and walk to the kitchen. I have a few things prepared, such as croissants, fruit, and jam, but still must make the coffee. It makes me shudder to think anyone would drink coffee from a convenience store.

For the next several minutes while I brew coffee, I try not to think of how she pronounced Damiano's name in her American accent, or whether she's even aware that Damiano died from the virus her ancestor introduced to the world.

Probably she doesn't know, but it doesn't really matter, does it?

I carry a tray with the cappuccino and the croissants into the library, and find Evangeline sitting in front of the fire, her back to me. Her boots and hat are off, and her still-damp hair cascades over her shoulders.

"Are you warming up?" I set the tray on a nearby leather ottoman and sink onto the floor next to her.

"Yes, this feels incredible. Thank you."

"You haven't even tried my coffee. Here."

She carefully takes the cup from my hands and sips. "Oh, god, that is so much better than the 7-Eleven coffee." Her laughter fills the room and I can't help but smile. "You must think I'm like a redneck or a hick for drinking that."

"Nope, you're simply American." Her mouth drops open and I laugh. "Kidding. Just kidding."

"Well, we all can't be European royalty, or whatever you are."

"Is that what you think? That I'm royalty?" I stare at her, amused. She really is refreshing and lovely.

Her shoulder lifts and she takes a sip of her coffee, then swallows. "I don't know what to think. I was pretty shocked that you came by and left a note at my dorm, especially after everything last night. I'm not used to men being this...interested, this quickly."

"Really? I find that difficult to believe."

"Why?"

"Because you're gorgeous. You're also funny. I would think you have to beat back guys with a stick."

"You're very good at flattery, you know that? Is that an Italian thing?"

I smirk in her direction. "Perhaps."

She takes a few more sips of coffee and stares at the fire. "I almost didn't come. I was supposed to meet my brother for breakfast but he stood me up."

Prickles of awareness wash over me. John Ransom is in Boston? Oh, this is so much easier than I anticipated. "Oh, really?"

She nods. "He showed up, out of the blue, last night after you left."

As she describes how they went for a slice of pizza in Kenmore Square, I have to remind myself to remain calm. To not project any emotion. To not show how eager I am for more information.

"Yeah, it was the first time I've seen him in so long. He's been over in London. I guess he's leaving Boston soon, I don't know. We used to be close, but now..." Her tongue darts out and licks a drop of milk on the corner of her mouth, a move that's achingly sensual.

"Now you're not close?" I reach across her and take a grape from the tray, pretending to be only mildly interested.

"Pfft. I don't know what we are. He's changed a lot. Family's really complicated, you know?"

"So why didn't you stay at your dorm this morning, in hopes your brother showed up? Maybe he was late, and you missed him." I'm hoping for further revelation, another nugget of detail. Something that will lead me to him.

She sets her cup down on the tray and twists her body so she's staring directly at me. We're only a foot apart, but I feel a need to close the distance in some way. It's too soon for a kiss, although that would be satisfying. So I reach out to stroke the top of her hand with my thumb.

"I live my own life. My brother had the chance to see me, and didn't show. I waited almost an hour. When I got your note, I felt..."

We stare into each other's eyes, and for the briefest of seconds, I think of how I'd be content to look at her beautiful face for a thousand years.

Even I can sense the temperature rise in the room, and my resolve to pump her for information is fading, replaced with the overwhelming desire to feel her lips once again.

"You're not finishing a lot of your sentences today," I murmur while continuing to caress the smooth skin of her hand. "Why is that? What did you feel, Evangeline?"

"I felt. Ah. Drawn to you. Drawn here. I don't know why. Well, actually, I'm lying. I do know why."

"Tell me," I whisper.

She leans into me, her eyelids fluttering shut. For the second time in twenty-four hours, she kisses me first.

# Desire, Part One

Why am I kissing Matteo?

Why did I throw myself at him not a half hour after arriving?

Why do I crave the feel of his lips against mine?

We kiss for several long seconds, slow and languid, as the flames nearby crackle and flare. He slides his hand over the side of my neck and jaw, and his touch leaves a trail of heat. He digs his fingers into my flesh. Yes. Yes. Yes. This is what I want. This, I could become addicted to.

Perhaps I already am.

His tongue finds mine, swiping and teasing. I gently bite his bottom lip. He bites mine in response and I suck in a breath, anticipating the other bites to come.

"Did you like that?" he whispers against my mouth.

"I did."

"Do you like it rough?"

I don't exactly know what to respond. Whenever I've made out with a guy, I've enjoyed some mild hair pulling and the occasional pinning of my wrists. Mostly I've loved the visual of a man's bigger hands trapping mine.

But this man, this vampire, likely has a whole other definition of rough.

"I think I do," I finally say.

"That's good to hear." His response is barely audible, strained, even.

Then he stops, and puts his forehead against mine, and sighs.

"So this is why you came over? To fuck?" he murmurs.

I sit back, needing space, needing to collect myself. My heart's thrashing wildly, and not just because of the kiss. Something about being here, in this library, with that fire, in a beautiful Beacon Hill townhouse makes everything seem so much more intimate.

Can I admit that I would fuck him here and now? It seems so out of character for me. But I don't want just sex...

I lick my lips. "I don't know. I came here because you invited me, remember? And I was intrigued. And because I wanted to see you."

Needed to see you.

He traces my kneecap with his index finger. "Interesting. Can you tell me more?"

I huff out a little laugh. "What is this, therapy? That's something my mother would say."

His right eyebrow lifts. "Oh?"

"Yeah, she's a therapist." I pause. "It's a pain in the ass because she's always asking me to get in touch with my feelings."

"So you don't like to talk about feelings?" He takes a sip of his coffee and scoots next to me, so we're both sitting side-by-side. His instant, friend zone voice, makes me wonder if I've killed the mood.

I lift a shoulder. "It's not that. I guess I'm feeling something different around you and..."

My voice trails off. It's never a good idea to tell a guy that you're into them this early. God, we've only seen each other twice. What the hell am I doing? My cheeks flare with heat, and not because of the nearby fireplace.

The whispers of my mother's advice when I went off to college — don't be too interested in a man, you have to play hard to get — echo in my brain.

"And?" Matteo asks.

"Why do you care so much about what I'm feeling? Most guys don't."

He lets out a genuine laugh. "I think you'll find that I'm not like most men, Evangeline."

Well, duh, I want to say. But don't. Because it's quite important that I don't let on about the obvious. That he's a vampire, and I want him to turn me into a vampire. The sex is just a bonus, not the end game.

We sip coffee in awkward silence.

I didn't think it would be this difficult to persuade a seemingly horny vampire guy to bite me. Thoughts race through my mind, all centered around the refrain of what's wrong with me, and do I smell or taste bad? Why the hell isn't he jumping my bones? Isn't the scent of my blood enticing enough? Shame, shame, shame.

I set the coffee back down.

"I'm attracted to you," I blurt. Sometimes I do that when I'm nervous. Kerri calls it word vomiting. "That's the truth. I know that probably makes me less alluring or something, but whatever."

In a flash, he wraps his hand around the back of my neck and tugs me toward him. The move is so sudden, so quick, that I don't have time to gasp. Our faces are an inch apart, and I can feel my heartbeat in my throat.

"Evangeline." His voice is both a low growl, and a command, and in that moment I realize that I'll do anything this man asks. "Never apologize for your desires."

# Desire, Part Two

We're breathing in tandem now, and I suspect we're both thinking the same thing.

Where is this going?

"What do you desire?" I whisper.

"For now? For today? Or in general?"

"For now." Maybe it's the light of the fire in this dark room, the way the shadows and the light of the flames play against his skin, but today I'm noticing small details of his face. Like his nose, which is subtly crooked and leads me to believe he was involved in something violent. Like the way his jaw is sharp enough to slice me in two.

It would be interesting to know what he desires in the long term, what goals and dreams an immortal like him has.

But for now, I want only one answer. "What do you desire right now?" I ask.

"You," he says.

That's exactly what I want to hear. He repeats it. "You, Evangeline. I want you. Naked and spread open right on this rug. You, for the taking. You, for hours, letting me do whatever I desire. And I have a lot of desires."

The red glint in his eyes sends a frisson of fear through me. It's an intense, almost furious stare, unblinking and unwavering. I have never been around a man who looks at me like this, who seems to want me so much that it angers him.

And I probably never will.

Knowing this is all supremely fucked up on my part, I do the only thing that's in my heart: I lean forward and devour Matteo's mouth again. He even tastes good. Some guys have slightly funky breath or taste a little sour. Not Matteo. He tastes mostly like nothing, with a subtle hint of coffee and chocolate.

I've also noticed that his skin temperature is different than mine. Not corpse-like cold, but a pleasing coolness that both quenches my own heat and makes me flare with want.

He laughs softly as I trail kisses down his neck.

"What?' I ask.

"I love how fucking eager you are. It's a huge turn-on."

"Show me how huge." Something about his brutal exterior makes me want to challenge him, like I'm playing with the devil himself.

Considering what Matteo really is, that's probably an apt description. But I don't care, because now he's kissing me back, pulling me toward him and lying back on the sumptuous scarlet rug so that I'm on top of him.

He sits up, and we're suddenly in a jumble of limbs and lips, with me grinding against him while he pushes my black sweater up my body and over my head. I feel like I'm burning on the inside, while my skin singes from the proximity of the fireplace and of him.

Thoughts tumble through my brain as frenzied as our movements.

Is this the moment where he'll bite me? Where he'll drain my body of all blood? Or will sex come first? I kind of hope it does.

"Take off your bra, I've never been good with those damn things," he mutters while unbuttoning his white shirt.

I laugh and rock against his hips. I can feel his hardness underneath our layers of clothes. His leather pants are making me glide against him, and a delicious thrill goes through me and coalesces between my legs. I'm wetter than I was last night, which I didn't think possible.

"What's so funny?" Even his smirk looks dangerous.

My hands are behind my back, on my bra clasp. I don't shed my bra right away, partially because I want to tease him, and because I think my breasts look pretty damned sexy and I want to savor this moment. I've never felt so...desirable, and it's quite heady. And the fact that this hot vampire guy is complaining about mundane bra clasps makes me giggle even more.

"You seem like such a practiced seducer. I figure you'd know how to unhook a bra with one hand."

His smirk turns to a laugh and he undoes two buttons on his white shirt. "A practiced seducer, hunh?"

He cups my breasts and squeezes. In the span of a millisecond he yanks at the fabric. My pretty black lace bra is in tatters and he flings it into the fireplace, which consumes the lingerie.

"You just ripped my best bra." I feign a gasp.

"I'll buy you a new one," he grinds out as his mouth finds my right nipple.

By the time he runs his tongue over the stiff peak, the bra is ancient history, and I'm arching my back, thrusting myself toward him like the wanton slut I apparently am.

Actually, I don't know what I am in the moment, other than his.

# Sympathy for the Devil

Matteo is achingly gentle as he sits up and pushes me onto the rug. I'm on my back, vulnerable and overpowered, and I don't give a damn.

For a few minutes, he hovers over me, with one hand propping himself up and the other lightly skimming my skin. I'm almost writhing now, needing more of his touch. He's not giving it yet, though, not bestowing his long fingers or his beautiful mouth. Stingy bastard. I want it all. Tease. That's what he's doing.

Teasing me mercilessly.

I let out an impatient little grunt.

"What?" he whispers, his eyes meeting mine. That smirk is back, paired with the slow roll of my nipple between his thumb and forefinger. "What do you want?"

I shudder in a breath and shake my head.

He pauses, removing his hand from my breast, and I almost scream in frustration. "Do you want me to stop?"

"No, hell no," I hiss, leaning up to kiss him.

But he evades me with a chuckle and sits up. "Oh, that wasn't a stop noise. It was a, how do you say it? Horny noise?"

I giggle. "A horny frustrated noise."

"Let's do something about that, then. First," he moves to my feet and begins unlacing my boots. "These need to come off."

He takes his sweet time unlacing them, then slips one off my foot. I want to just kick and strip away everything touching my body and fuse myself to him, but he has other plans.

"Cute socks," he observes, holding up one of my feet. They're black-and-white striped. "And look at these little feet with the black nail polish."

He runs a finger down the sole of my foot. Normally I'm ticklish, but it seems that every touch of his sends an electric current through my body.

"Other foot," I say.

"You're quite demanding." He bites his lip and removes my other shoe and sock. "And what's all this?"

He tugs at my skirt-leggings combo.

"Layers. It's cold out."

"Are you still cold?"

No. I might spontaneously combust. I shake my head.

"So is this a one piece or what?" He pretends to lift my skirt, inspecting the fabric.

"Ugh, no. It's two." I push both the skirt and leggings down, and shove everything down my legs until I'm only in a pair of black lace panties. I settle back on the floor, my legs tightly closed.

"Ohhh." The word comes out as an appreciative growl. But instead of lowering himself down upon me, he sits on his knees and stares. For a second I think he's going to get up and leave, and then he undoes the final two buttons on his white shirt, slowly stripping it off.

Maybe I'd been in a fog last night, or it's something about this sumptuous, regal-looking décor. But he looks more sinewy and sexy today in the light of the fire, slightly older and hard. His collar-bone accentuates his muscles and his cheekbone highlights his pouty mouth. He's muscular but not ripped.

"Aren't you going to..." my voice fades as he slowly unbuckles his belt and pulls it out of the loops of his leather pants.

"Going to what? Fling myself on top of you? Evangeline," he lowers himself to kiss my nose then maddeningly sits back up, "what kind of men have you been with prior to me?"

I huff out a laugh. "Well, the last guy I made out with was two months ago."

Matteo's eyes flare red. I wonder if he knows that I can see the red in his eyes, or if he thinks I'm a full human who cannot. "Two months ago. Hmm."

I skim my hands over my breasts, then squeeze. "Yeah that guy went like this." I pantomime a squeezing motion on my boobs. "Then he said, honk, honk. And that's when I kicked him out of my room."

Matteo laughs, and it's the first time I've seen him genuinely mirthful. With his hands on his spread thighs, he tips his head back and chuckles, and the sound is so wonderful that I have to laugh, too.

While still grinning, he nudges my hands aside and cups my breasts with his cool palms.

"I'm glad to know I won't have a lot of competition with the college boys."

"Hardly."

"Good. Because I'm a very competitive man, and above all, I like to win."

"That brings me back to my original question. Why are you taking this so slow?" I regret the words as soon as they're out of my mouth. Why am I so eager for sex — or death? Somehow between the kissing of my nipples and the stripping off of clothes I've forgotten that he's a fucking vampire.

He brushes a lock of hair out of my face, and again skims his hands over my body, stopping at my stomach. He seems to spend a lot of time staring at my breasts, or maybe I'm imagining that.

"When you look at a beautiful painting, do you breeze by with just a glance? Or do you take your time and savor?"

I snicker.

"What?" he asks, tilting his head.

"That's a really good line. Bravo."

"Ouch. That hurts." He clutches his hands to his chest as if he's wounded. "I'm serious. I don't believe in rushing sex. Ever."

"I'm sure you do believe that. But you could've fooled me last night."

"You modern women are so impatient," he murmurs, almost to himself, and a tantalizing thrill goes through me. There. He just acknowledged that he's lived a long time. "And last night was... unusual."

"Yeah. Sure was."

"I like looking at you." He traces a ring around my belly button, then trails his fingertips to the edge of my panties. "And I want to see all of you."

With his index finger, he slowly tugs the edge of my panties down, over my hipbone. I'm breathing hard now, because he's just so damned intense. All of my wisecracks and comebacks have evaporated.

Slowly, he nudges my panties lower, so that part of me is exposed. He pauses and dips his head, kissing the spot between my belly button and where my hair begins. I rake in a breath at the feel of his lips.

He lifts his head. "You like that?"

I swallow and nod.

"Good. There will be more. Count on it."

He sits up and slides the panties down my legs. I assist by lifting my hips, and he tosses them aside, near a velvet ottoman. Then he stares at me, his gaze raking over every intimate part of my body.

"Fucking beautiful," he whispers.

My legs are still fused together. Now, I've been touched — fingered, as Kerri calls it — by guys before. But never have I felt so exposed as I do today.

Matteo rests his hands on my knees and nudges them apart. I butterfly my legs so that I'm showing him my all.

"Just like that, Evangeline. My god. Look at you." He captures his full bottom lip in his mouth and stares between my legs with those glowing red eyes.

"Can I touch you?" The hoarse, rough tone is back, and combine with how respectful he's being, it's making me melt.

"Yes," I say clearly, not wanting there to be any question about what I desire.

With a gossamer touch, he skims his thumb over my labia, so soft and subtle that I whimper.

"You're already so wet."

Wet doesn't even cover it. I'm soaked, more than I've ever been. Probably messy, but I don't dare look because I don't want to feel shame or embarrassment right now. All I can see are his intense eyes, his dark brow, his strained muscles, as if it's taking great effort to hold himself back from attacking me.

His thumb delves a little deeper into me, then his fingers take over, skimming between my folds. My clit throbs with need. Never have I felt such want as I do now, and it's making me go mad because I can't control my feelings.

I squirm, wanting a firmer touch, wanting him to take the ache away, wanting those cool fingers of his to eliminate the heat circulating in my veins.

He gently rubs my clit in circles, then slides his middle finger into me. I respond by spreading my legs wide and pushing myself into him.

"Why am I like this with you?" I blurt, in a whisper.

"Like what?"

"Needy. Horny. Slutty."

"I don't know, but I'm glad you are."

He adds a second finger and with great control, moves in and out of me, the wetness making a subtle, dirty sound that's drowned out by the crackling of the fire. I'm close to detonating, and I know that only a graze of my clit will bring me to orgasm.

A wicked grin spreads on his face. "You can't come just yet, amore. I'm just getting started with you. Try to control yourself, please."

# Drink You Dry

I'm dimly aware that it's daytime. Is it even noon? It's a Sunday, I know that much. Normally I'd be out shopping with Kerri, or grabbing coffee, or studying. Today my world has shifted, as if I've stepped into a parallel universe. The darkness of the room and the warm glow of the fire makes it feel like nighttime. It's a huge change from my boring dorm, and the fact that I'm lying here, naked in a private library, is decadent and dirty.

But I'm not ashamed, possibly because Matteo's staring at me with something bordering on reverence. Although maybe I should be. I'm sure there are many people who would think less of me if they knew where I was, and what I was doing, with a man like Matteo.

He's trailing his fingers over my skin, causing flares of desire to surge in me, stoking the embers of need. I whimper when he circles my bellybutton, squirm when he brushes lightly over my pussy, shimmy my hips in his direction.

All this while he's wearing nothing but those black leather pants and a self-satisfied smirk.

"You think this is funny or something?" I ask in a mock, accusatory tone. "You're teasing me."

He stops touching me and taps his index finger on his lips. "Funny. Hmm. I find this a lot of things, but not funny."

His fingers find the inside of my thigh and I suck in a breath. No one's touched me there before, and while it's not precisely where I want him to stroke, it's making me wetter than I ever thought possible.

"Hasn't anyone ever teased you before, Evangeline?"

The truth, of course, is no. The guys I've been with have been either inept or aggressive, and often both. Which is why I'm still a virgin. If a guy can't get me as wet as I can get myself, why would I have sex with him? I open my mouth to explain this to Matteo but his hand is between my legs, tracing the seam of my sex.

I sigh my response. "No. No one's teased me."

His thumb is brushing my outer lips, so close to my clit. I'm practically humming with horniness, and if I weren't so frustrated I'd want to laugh about it.

"Maybe you should be eased more often." His voice is a low murmur, and again his gaze is leveled at my pussy. "Because the more I tease you, the wetter you seem to get."

"Imagine that," I say in a sarcastic tone.

He chuckles and dips a finger inside me, pausing to slowly stroke my clit. I shut my eyes so I can lose myself in the sensation, but that doesn't feel right either, because I want to keep looking at him. At his brutal beauty, at the way he's staring at me as if I captivate him.

I don't think I've ever captivated a man before. Sure, I've given them hard-ons and briefly enticed them enough to awkwardly beg for sex. But none have looked at me like Matteo is —like I'm both a priceless work of art and an object that he wants to defile in the most filthy way.

While his hand plays between my legs, he stretches on his side, next to me, so we're both prone on the rug.

I shift to face him, so I can kiss him, but he makes a tsk sound with his tongue.

"Shh. I'm not done here."

"I... what..." my voice dies in my throat when he increases the pressure while circling my clit. I'm pulsing and throbbing and practically quaking, I'm so close to an orgasm.

"You what, Evangeline? What? Are you going to let go?" His lips hover against my ear. "Give it to me."

He plunges two fingers inside me, then slowly withdraws them, skimming through my wetness and around my clit. He does this over and over, so practiced and expert that I wonder how he knows this is what truly turns me on.

And so, I let go. I dissolve against his fingers, my orgasm taking my breath away. But he's not done rubbing, and I pulse and orgasm again. I gasp aloud when I realize that he's trailing his tongue down my stomach, moving down my body so his mouth is on my clit.

I'm literally orgasming against his tongue now, grinding myself into his face and crying out, digging my nails into his scalp.

His tongue assaults my already throbbing clit, and he laps at my flesh, inspiring a strangled noise to build low in my throat. I can't believe how good this feels; there are truly no words. And the fact that he brought me to orgasm then decided to go down on me while I was still in the middle of it all?

Shocking.

He's now licking me fiercely, punctuating with small, gentle bites of my pussy, occasionally replacing his tongue with his fingers and pressing his mouth to my inner thigh.

Two thoughts hit me through the fog of my orgasm. The first is that I remember he's a vampire. Somehow that got lost during all the fingering and licking and orgasming.

The second is that vampires don't necessarily need the jugular to feed. They can also drink blood from a femoral artery, which is the major pathway that blood travels from the lower limbs to the heart. It's about two inches from my pussy, and it's exactly where Matteo is nibbling softly as he gives me yet another orgasm with his fingers.

"Fuck, you taste incredible," he mutters. "I want to drink you dry."

This, of course, gives me an idea. Which is pretty impressive considering I'm in a sex fog and my pussy's still quivering from the orgasms.

Our eyes meet and I manage a grin through my heavy breaths. "Will you do something that I really like?" I ask.

He licks my inner thigh. "Of course. What's that?"

"Will you bite me? Hard? Right here?" I tap on my inner thigh and he looks up at me, his eyes flashing a deep, intense scarlet.

His lips, which glisten with my juices, part. His four sharp fangs glint in the light of the fire.

"Please?" I beg.

# *Blood Scent*

Am I hearing her correctly? She wants me to what?

I flutter kisses on her inner thigh as my thumb glides through her tantalizing, glistening, wet folds. Evangeline is as delicious as she is beautiful. I should have said no to all of this, though. All of the kisses, all of the touches, every single plunge of my fingers inside her juicy, delectable cunt.

Something about her inspires weakness in me, and I can't figure out why.

Her fingers work into my scalp and she subtly moves my face into her flesh. If only I could do what she wants. What does she want, exactly? She has no idea what she's toying with, here in my darkened library lair.

This situation requires clarification, because I think she just begged me to bite her on the thigh. That can't be right. Most women don't want that, I've discovered over the years.

"You want me to—"

"Bite me. On the thigh. It's, ah, my kink."

Oh dear god. What am I to do now? It's already taking a herculean effort not to bite her, not to drink her blood. The tantalizing, copper-sweet smell—her blood scent— is embedded deeply in my brain just from kissing and licking her, and all of this spells certain ruin for me in so many ways.

My tongue takes on a life of its own, running up her inner thigh. Her skin tastes on par with the most delicious dishes I've tasted; sweet with a twinge of salt, smooth with a hint of butter. I almost feel like I want to claw out of my skin because I'm craving her blood and my cock is as hard as a diamond.

Her blood would taste incredible. That thought, and the scent hiding in her veins under her skin, makes me groan aloud from sheer desperation.

"Does that mean you'll bite me?" she whispers fiercely.

I dig my fingers into her hips, pulling her closer. Fuck.

I brush my lips against the soft skin of her inner thigh, wanting nothing more than to sink my fangs into her. The thigh isn't my preferred location—I'm a traditionalist and like the neck. But she's a special case, and I'm sure drinking from any part of her would be delectable.

But feeding from a half vampire-half human is prohibited by my superiors, and what am I going to do once I've consumed her blood? Allow her to be a vampire? That's a terrible fate for someone like Evangeline, and a harsh punishment for me.

And yet, I don't think I could bring myself to ram a stake into her heart to prevent her from becoming one of us, one of the undead. It's what I usually do with my victims, after I've finished feeding. This is to ensure they don't live a cursed existence for all of eternity.

No, I can't do that, either.

My tongue continues its slow journey up her thigh, and I pause, tempted to strike. My rational side, which often wins out, tells me to wait a few minutes. See if I can collect myself.

So instead of biting her, I shift my head a few inches, so that my tongue is deep in her beautiful pussy.

What an exquisite sacrifice.

I spread her apart with my thumbs and pull up her clitoral hood so I can gain better access to that bundle of nerves.

She's mewling now, opening her legs wider. It's sheer torment, because I haven't wanted to fuck or feed a woman this bad in centuries. Perhaps ever.

"Again? You're going to make me come again?" she gasps.

Oh dearest Evangeline, I'd make you orgasm for eternity if I could.

"Mmm-hmm," I hum into her flesh.

"Okay, I guess that's fine."

I raise my head and one eyebrow. "Fine? It's merely fine? I can stop if you'd like and we can resume drinking coffee."

She makes the cutest little pout and a noise of indignation. "You'd better not."

I chuckle and return to her sex, licking and stroking and sucking. It's like I've known for years what makes this woman tick, which is unusual.

Women usually are a mystery to me, but Evangeline is like an open book, one that was written only for me.

# *Lust*

I don't know much about Evangeline. I don't know her favorite aria or her preferred reading genre or even what she likes to eat (other than possibly pizza, and I suspect that it's terrible here in Boston, compared to my beloved pizza in Napoli).

Given that she's a modern woman, and that modern women—hell, all women— confound me, I wouldn't hazard a guess at her preferences. But there is a vibration between us, something that seems to flow with ease.

Maybe it's sexual tension? Maybe my years-long celibacy has somehow affected my judgment? I almost laugh out loud because I'm thinking this while my face is buried between her legs.

We've known each other for less than twenty-four hours, and most of that time we've indulged in our physical desires. Not that there's anything wrong with that — as Damiano used to say, we might be undead, but we still need pleasure. "Why not indulge," he'd ask, then laugh.

Vampires live a life of tedious, grasping eternity, he'd add, but at least the occasional orgasm makes it somewhat tolerable. And to be sure, I have indulged from time to time. I try to keep sex separate from feeding, because one is sustenance and the other is practically spiritual.

God knows I want to indulge in this woman who is splayed before me. Fortunately for the both of us, I fed recently, so I don't need to satiate that particular need today. If I hadn't, I would've probably already drained Evangeline dry.

Horniness and hunger are a painful combination for a vampire.

But there are a few other problems that I can't overlook, even if her pussy tastes delicious and her body feels perfect in my hands, like clay ready to be molded into a masterpiece.

I ease away from her pussy, replacing my tongue with my thumb. The added pressure on her clit drives her wild, I've discovered, and that makes my dick positively throb with need. So. Fucking. Satisfying.

But my dick needs to stay out of this. I'm aware of that fact. Sadly, my dick is one of the many problems right now.

Vampires like me aren't supposed to fuck or feed from halflings. This is codified in The Council's rules, ones that I agreed to hundreds of years ago. I'm treading on thin ice by kissing and stroking Evangeline, although I suspect the council would spare me because this is a means to an end.

At least that's what I'm telling myself. I'm doing a terrible job of finding out about her brother, although I suppose that will come later.

"Please, Matteo? Your tongue?" she whispers, as if helpless.

"Of course," I murmur, licking her once more. She sighs in such an indulgent way that I want to keep this up all day long.

Back to the problems...

She doesn't know that I know.

As I bring Evangeline to the brink of another orgasm with my tongue, my mind races with thoughts.

She doesn't know that I'm aware she's a half-vampire, half-human. And she doesn't know I'm a vampire. This is unsurprising, because halflings like her don't have a sophisticated sense of smell or taste, and their intuition isn't as developed as a full vampire's. I've heard the human side takes over when halflings are in the presence of full-blooded vampires, which means their senses are stunted.

I have a vague memory of being human and recall my lack of awareness in those areas.

At least, I don't think Evangeline is aware I'm a vampire; I've only met a few like her in my long life, and frankly, have tried to distance myself from them. Halflings are often physically stunning, like she is, but problematic.

Like she is. And normally I despise problems, so...

If she did know what I am, she'd be far more afraid. It's my understanding that halflings have a deep fear of full vampires.

If she knows what I am, she wouldn't be begging me to bite her thigh. She wouldn't be thrusting herself into my mouth, wouldn't be pleading for me to give her relief over and over.

Thank god she ceased her pleas to bite her thigh; I think my oral abilities have made that particular request vanish.

As I lick and suck, I slip two fingers inside her, seeking that elusive, inner spot that will blow her mind. I can only imagine those human cretins she's been with have no idea what a G-spot is, much less how to find it.

I subtly move my fingers inside her and lift my head. She peeks through her fingers. "What are you doing to me? Maybe you should stop—"

As much as I want to destroy her brother — and possibly her, if she's on his side — I won't resort to sexual violence. That's a no-go as far as I'm concerned, in any circumstances. I slide my two fingers out of her and move up her body, kissing along the way. "You want me to stop?"

"No. Yes. I ... I don't know," she mumbles.

I gently clasp her wrists and pry her hands off her face. "What's wrong?"

Her face is flushed red, her eyes wide and panicked, her lips pink and kiss-stung. She's like a portrait of beauty, of unbridled lust, of fear and longing.

"I... I think I've had too many orgasms. I'm numb down there. I think we need to give her a little break." She dissolves into a giggle and folds into my chest, instantly charming me with her girlishness.

Her earlier sarcastic exterior seems to have crumbled with the scraps of affection I've thrown her way.

I kiss her forehead. "Absolutely. We don't want you numb in such an important area. We'd like to be able to use it again."

She laughs again, tips her head back and lets out a mirthful sound that's up there with birds singing and champagne bubbles popping. I can't help but be affected by her, although I'm aware I shouldn't succumb to her many charms.

She could be every bit as dangerous as her brother, although I doubt it. She's like a particularly eager kitten, not a killer predator.

Evangeline runs a finger down my bare chest. "How about I make you feel good?"

Her hand finds its way to my crotch and she presses on my erection, evident under the leather pants.

She licks her lips. "Please? It would make me so happy to, you know. Suck. Please?"

Why can't I resist her when she says this word? "Is that what you want?"

She nods, her eyes big and shining.

"Okay. I happen to prefer something other than lying on the floor for that, so..." I move stealthily to a nearby red velvet chair and sit, spreading my legs.

She crawls a few feet toward me, her pale skin glowing in the light of the fire. Her hair is wild and matted, the color of the flames. When she settles between my legs on her knees, she looks up.

We stare at each other as I slowly unbutton and unzip my pants. Her eyes drift downward as she watches me stroke myself, then she glances back up.

"You're big."

I lift a shoulder. "I guess."

With a grin, she leans forward, hands on my knees. I angle my dick into her mouth, and the second she licks it, I clasp her hair in one hand and exhale. Hell yes, sweet Evangeline.

She takes the entire tip into her mouth, and it's the most exquisite feeling. Like nothing I've experienced before.

"Take it all in," I groan.

She does, and I tip my head back, reveling in the sensation. My balls tighten, and a fluttering surge spreads through my groin.

And then, a thought slams into me:

Evangeline is my mate.

I don't know where the thought has come from, or why. I've never had it with any other woman, and it strikes a column of fear down my spine. It's so unsettling that I grip her hair harder, which inspires her to moan while deep throating me.

I look down at her and only one word is in my thoughts as I take in her curvy ass, the slope of her back, the grace of her spine.

Mine.

No fucking way. She can't be. Can she? I'd always heard from other vampires that discovering your mate usually happened during a sex act, when one least expected.

Panic slices through me.

I need to be alone to process. This is all wrong, and we must stop. Now.

I must talk myself out of this stupid notion. My lust turns to ice as fear takes over. Worried that my dick is about to deflate in her mouth — which would be supremely embarrassing and impossible to explain — I pull her up by her hair. It will be better for both of us if I end this swiftly.

"Evangeline," I say harshly. "You need to leave, now."

# Shame and Sorrow

I look up at him, my mouth open and wet. Until a second ago, I was having the best time. I'd felt sated and sensual and yeah, powerful, as I slid his hard cock between my lips.

I thought was loving everything. All signs pointed to his satisfaction. The way he let out a desperate, groaning growl. How he stroked my cheek as I took him into my mouth. When he whispered, "just like that, Evangeline baby, fuck yes," in that Italian accent.

The way he'd seemed to revel in my body, treating it like it was an object worthy of worship, not something to be used and discarded.

A grumble of confusion escapes my throat. "What? What's wrong? Did I do something wr-"

His grip on my hair tightens. My scalp stings and I reach for his hand while whining an ow sound.

"Stop! You're hurting me, Matteo."

His eyes are no longer glowing red, but a harsh, icy blue. He releases my hair and awkwardly pats me on top of my head, like a dog. "I'm sorry. You. Need. To. Leave."

"But..." I sit back on my heels and watch as he tucks himself back into his pants then rises to his feet.

He shakes his head. "I'll wait by the door while you dress."

His tone is as cold as I feel inside.

Stunned, my gaze follows Matteo as he stalks out of the room. What the hell just happened? Tears well in my eyes. Shame, anger, confusion swirl in my brain, making my heart pound as I wrap my arms around my bare midsection. My nipples, pink and raw from his attention, are no longer peaked and stiff. I'm sticky and gross between my legs, and the memory of him making me that wet is no longer a pleasant one — it's deeply humiliating.

I'm naked, vulnerable and freaked out. My teeth begin to chatter, as if I'm sitting in a snowbank and not a cozy, dark library. Even the roaring fire doesn't warm my flesh. Crap, I have to get out of here. This guy's unpredictable. Possibly worse than I ever imagined. I knew vampires could be emotional, mercurial, even. But what guy in his right mind halts a blowjob?

I scramble to gather my clothes. I swipe tears off my cheeks and remind myself to put on my underwear first. Where is my bra? Oh, right. He threw it into the fire hours ago.

Fucking awesome. He destroyed my favorite bra, gave me the best orgasms I'll probably ever have in my life, and then rejected me while I was sucking his dick.

Well, this is a new low.

A million thoughts go through my head, all with me in the starring role as the guilty party. Could he tell I'm a virgin, and didn't want to deal with that? Even so, I've given blowjobs before, and no one's ever complained. Did I accidentally bite him? I didn't think so.

He seemed so into it. So into me. What did I do wrong?

I suck in a breath and realize that my mouth now feels dry. The mug of coffee he'd made for me sits on an end table, and I reach for it while only in my leggings, skirt and bra. The liquid is cold and bitter now, not warm and nurturing as before. Whatever. I gulp it down and immediately regret it, because my stomach churns uncomfortably, as if I'm digesting pure acid.

"Fuck," I whisper. This is so profoundly confusing. Matteo was the first man I'd truly enjoyed being with sexually — and I could've sworn he wanted to feed on me.

I was so close to getting everything I wanted, and now, I have nothing but humiliation and embarrassment. I swallow a few times, trying to get the thick lump of tears out of my throat.

Hurriedly, I pull on my sweater, anxious that I'm taking too long. I pull on my socks and boots, then reach for my purse on a nearby chair. Because I'm shaking so much, I accidentally spill everything between the chair and an end table.

"Dammit," I hiss while scooping everything up, jamming it back into my bag.

I again swipe away the tears off my cheeks and take a deep, fortifying breath before I step into the hall.

Matteo's near the door, leaning against the wall, holding my wool coat. His posture is rigid, and his eyes are closed.

I stalk up to him, a twinge of anger cutting through all the other emotions, and grab my jacket from his hand.

His eyelids slap open. "I'm sor-"

"Save your apologies." Of course this is the time when I can't find my sleeve, and I flail with my jacket. "Sorry."

"Here, let me help you." He goes to hold my jacket.

"No. Don't bother." I'm trying not to escalate the situation by saying something sharp like fuck you or what the hell is wrong with you. I finally manage to get one arm through the sleeve, and I give up on the other, letting my jacket hang half off me in a pathetic twist.

Our eyes meet. To my surprise, there's a flicker of emotion there. Sadness? Confusion? He swallows, and his brow furrows, as if he's about to say something. As if he's as perplexed as I am.

This only makes me want to cry, and I'll be damned if I do that in front of him.

I shake my head and yank open the door. Or try to. It's locked. I am a bumbling idiot.

"Uh, sorry," he mumbles, reaching past me to undo the locks. His nearness and his smell — a heady scent of his cologne, coffee, and us — washes over me. I'm practically dizzy with the memory of him touching and kissing me, and it's all too overwhelming.

Fuck him.

Without saying a word, I step outside and run down the steps of the brownstone. It's somehow still daytime, and the bright sunshine belies the frigid air.

I want to look back to see if Matteo is watching me leave, but I don't. I can't. I won't give him that satisfaction. Somehow I manage to hold my head high and get my other arm into my coat sleeve.

But when I hear the sound of his door closing, I break into a run toward Beacon Street, and allow myself to sob as much as I want, not caring that people are gawking.

# Lovesick

I've been in bed for what seems like days — it's really only been a few hours since I staggered back to the dorm from Matteo's — when Kerri walks in. I'm lying under a thick, scratchy wool blanket, the sting of shame making my entire body feel raw and tender.

"Oh my God, Evan, did you hear the show today?" She shrugs off her leather jacket and deposits it on a nearby chair.

I reply with a grunt in the negative. Kerri is a DJ on our college radio station on Sunday afternoons, playing — what else — the latest in goth and punk, and usually I never miss the program. Sometimes I even go with her into the studio and help her pick out records and answer phones.

"Chris from Gang Green called in to request a song. He was soooo nice on the phone and I think we might get drinks later this week. Can you believe it?"

Normally the news that a locally famous punk rock singer wants to take my roommate out for drinks would be cause for celebration, but

I'm not in a mood to rejoice. Or discuss men. Or acknowledge guys even exist on Earth.

I stay silent, burrowing further under the covers.

"Hey, it's six, you want to head to the cafeteria for dinner and I'll tell you more about what Chris said? He has some hot band gossip."

"Mmph. No. Not hungry." My voice is muffled under the covers.

I shut my eyes, then feel the mattress near my feet sag with the weight of a person. I open one eye to see Kerri peering at me.

"You never nap. Are you sick?"

I sniffle and pull the green blanket over my head. "Yeah," I whine.

She flips the blanket down, revealing my puffy, pink face and red-rimmed eyes. "What the hell happened to you? You're never in bed before one in the morning. Is it the flu?"

Maybe I should lie and say yes, but Kerri will know instantly that I'm not sick from my scent. Damned vampires. I respond with a snortle, and wipe my nose on the sleeve of my sweatshirt.

Kerri strokes my hair. Under her tough-talking exterior she's really quite nurturing. "Is it your brother? Did you guys have a fight?"

I shake my head and flip onto my back, clutching a pillow to my chest. "John stood me up."

This tips me into another crying jag, thinking of my brother's anger last night, and his desire to kill the very thing that I just spent hours enjoying. To kill the one thing I want to be.

Suddenly everything seems so wrong and weird.

"Hey. Hey. What's going on? What happened? You're never like this. Is it your mom or dad? Did something happen?"

"It's Matteo," I say with a snorting honk of my nose.

"Matteo? The dude from last night?"

I nod and shudder in a breath.

"Did he come back to the room this morning after I left? What did he do to you? I swear to fuck I'll kill him if he hurt you." She pushes her hands through her hair. "Fucking Italian vampires. Wait. Did he..."

She hovers over me. "Let me see your neck."

I squirm away from her. "He didn't bite me."

"Did he touch you at all?" she demands.

This elicits a racking sob from me.

"Okay, what happened?" She stands up and grabs a pack of cigarettes off her desk, lighting one and cracking the window in between our beds. A little whoosh of frigid air soars into the room.

I press the heels of my hands into my eyes, wishing I could be anywhere but here right now. "He left a note here, asking me over for brunch. When John didn't show, I went over to Matteo's on a whim. Well, not his place. His friend' place on Beacon Hill."

Standing in the middle of the room, wearing a black tank top, black jeans, and heavy black boots, Kerri has the expression of a general who's about to go to war. She blows smoke out of her nose while scowling. "Go on."

"He made me coffee. We sat in his library, well, his friend's library. It was so beautiful. There was a fire in the fireplace, and red velvet chairs and so many books. Oh, and a real painting..." I let my voice trail off while sitting up.

"Okay..."

"And we got to, you know, fooling around. Making out. Getting naked."

"Uh-huh." Her eyes narrow as she approaches my bed and sits, cigarette in hand.

I bend my knees and wrap my arms around my legs. "It was incredible. He um, you know."

"No. I don't know. No euphamisms here, Evan. I need to know it all so I can decide whether to kick his ass."

This is the thing. Kerri is strong. And obviously, undead. Ass-kicking is her specialty, as she likes to remind me. Although I haven't seen real evidence of this aside from the occasional punch to a frat boy or skinhead's face in a mosh pit, I also wouldn't want to test her.

I scrunch my eyes shut. "I got naked, he fingered me, went down on me and everything was just peachy keen," I say in a sarcastic tone. "But I was giving him a blowjob, and he told me to leave. Oh god, it sounds even worse when I say it aloud."

Kerri runs her tongue over her teeth and stares at her cigarette. "That seems weird. Usually after guys blow their load they can't form a coherent thought or sentence for a while. Even vampire men are like that. But still. Dick move. I hate him."

"No, you don't understand. He told me to leave in the middle of the blowjob."

She takes a long drag of her cigarette while studying me. "Excuse me?"

"Yeah. That's why it was so mortifying. I was naked, on my knees, and he pulled my hair and told me to get out. Everything was awesome before that."

"He pulled your hair? Like in a kinky way?"

"No. It hurt. He let go after a second. He seemed angry."

Kerri's exhale surrounds us in cloud of clove-scented smoke. "Did you tell him that you're a halfling?"

"Nope."

"Did you tell him that you're aware he's a vampire?"

I shake my head. "As far as he knows, I'm just a horny college girl he met at a club, one who likes goth looking dudes in leather pants."

Kerri stares at the door, smoking, in silence. I'm too miserable to speak, and zone out, but after a few minutes, I pipe up.

"Why do you think he did that? Isn't that weird?"

She raises her eyebrows and contemplates the tip of her cigarette. "Weird? For a human, yes. For a vampire guy? Maybe not."

"I don't get it. Wouldn't he want me to suck him? Wouldn't he want to have sex? Bite me? Anything other than being rude and sending me away?"

She rises and crosses the room, stubbing out her cigarette in an ashtray. "I suspect he wanted all three of those things. Desperately. More than anything."

I let out a strangled groan. "So why did he have to embarrass and humiliate me, why ask me to leave? I would've stayed all day and night. We had such great chemistry. We laughed. We talked about art."

Kerri returns to my bed and plunks down. "Perhaps in between playing yuppie house on Beacon Hill, you two had far too much chemistry and he got scared. He didn't know what to do."

"That's ridiculous. Vampires have strong libidos. You've said it yourself. He didn't seem scared." But that flicker in his eyes as I left... that was a little odd.

"I'm sure he does have a strong libido. He gave off that vibe last night."

"Then what's the problem?" Kerri seems like she's not explaining everything, and I feel two steps behind.

She clears her throat. "I'm trying to tell you that perhaps your connection, your attraction, issue to, ah, fate, than a casual hookup."

"What? I don't get it."

Kerri snorts. "Jesus. Have you not been listening to me all these years? Vampires often search for their fated mates, so they can get avoid the hell of eternal life. It's one of the reasons why I sleep around. Okay, and I like sex."

"I know, I know. And once a vampire finds their fated mate, if they have a child together, they'll no longer be immortal, thus releasing them from their purgatory. I got it. That's my parents. So what?"

"So perhaps Matteo is under the impression that you're his mate. Maybe he knows more about you than you think. Maybe he's trying to save you, Evan. Or maybe he's not interested in finding his mate, and he's trying to save himself."

# Feeding

"Evan. It's eight-thirty. You getting up?" Kerri's normally raspy voice is uncharacteristically soft and my eyes flutter open, then closed.

"Not going to class today," I mumble, pulling the comforter away from my face.

I've been in bed since yesterday, since that disastrous visit to Matteo's house. I've only drank a can of Coca-Cola since, and skipped both dinner and breakfast at the dining hall. Shame and anger are still swirling in my gut, mixed with some old-fashioned sickness vibes.

Good times.

"I think you should get up and go."

I open my eyes in time to see Kerri looming over my bed, inspecting me. "Nope. I feel like shit."

"You'll feel better if you shower, put on some makeup, and walk across the street to class. Today's psychology, right? You always talk about how easy that is. You like the professor, too."

I don't respond, trying to remember what day it is. Monday? Yes, it's Monday. Which means early psych class, held closest to our dorm in the lecture hall across the street. It's held Mondays, Wednesdays and Fridays, and starts at nine. I could still make it, stumble out of the dorm and across the street.

But sleep and exhaustion press down on my body, and I'm physically unable to do what my mind is considering.

"My head feels like it's splitting in two. I think I have a fever." I follow up with a groan.

Kerri's arm extends downward, and her cool hand presses against my forehead. "You do feel warm. Why don't I bring you some breakfast?"

The cafeteria is in the bottom floor of the lecture hall. Kerri wouldn't have far to go. Since it's Monday, Kerri doesn't have class until ten. "You don't have to."

"Shut up. I'm going to run across the street. Don't move."

"Not planning to move ever again," I grumble, and I hear her footsteps, then the opening and shutting of the door. Physical exertion is not on my agenda.

I lapse back into a sweaty sleep, my emotions about Matteo still all over the place. Like last night, I dream of him, of his kisses, of his smooth skin, of those glowing eyes.

This truly sucks.

Sometime later, I wake with a start. Alarmed, I look around the room, briefly unaware of where I am.

Kerri's in the middle of the room, struggling to open one of those small cartons of cereal. "Fuck this plastic wrapping shit. Oh hey, good morning, sunshine! I got your favorite kind, the Froot Loops," she says in a sing-song. "You can eat it dry or I got some milk and a plastic bowl and spoon. Your choice."

"Don't want any."

"Come on, try to eat. Sit up. I'll feed you."

Exhausted, I haul myself up so I'm sitting against the wall. Having Kerri spoon feed me is beyond mortifying. "Dry. I'll try it dry. I'm not that sick."

"God, you look like shit. I'm worried about you." She hands me the little box of cereal.

"Thanks." I shake cereal into my palm.

"You're sure he didn't bite you anywhere?" Kerri sits on the side of my bed.

I let out a snort and shovel the handful of cereal into my mouth. "I think I'd have remembered that, sometime between the fingering and the throwing me out of the house. No bites. I tried to get him to. Begged, even."

She rolls her eyes. "Christ. Okay. It's just really weird you're sick immediately after hooking up with him. Usually when someone's turned they feel some flu-like symptoms. Or worse."

"It's probably because I walked home in the cold without buttoning my jacket. Or I just caught something."

"Hmm. Maybe you should go to the clinic." Her tone is one of disapproval. Because she's a vampire, Kerri never gets sick with colds or the flu. I, on the other hand, get a cold seemingly every other month when physically or mentally stressed. So this morning isn't much a of a surprise.

"I just need a day to sleep. I'm only missing one class, it's not a big deal." And it shouldn't be; I never miss lectures. Usually I power through even when ill, but not today.

"Okay. Well, I got you some juice, water, soda, and some trail mix. And one of those soup cup thingies that you like. I'm going to class. I'll check in after, though."

"Thanks. I appreciate it. I really do." My eyes go from Kerri to the cereal, which suddenly looks incredibly unappetizing. One of these days I'm going to stop eating sugar.

Kerri squeezes my foot under the covers and says goodbye, and struts out of the room. I attempt to munch another handful of cereal, but find it too sweet and dry.

That's when I remember how Matteo told me how sweet I tasted, and I cry myself to sleep.

# # #

It goes like this for two more days. I stay in bed, Kerri brings me food. I choke down more dry cereal and even a bit of chicken noodle soup she bought at a restaurant in Kenmore Square.

I cry, a lot. I'm not even sure why. Kerri just sighs and rubs my back until I fall into another sweat-soaked slumber. Sometimes she puts on WFNX on the radio, but when I hear songs that remind me of Matteo — pretty much anything by the Cure, which they play seemingly every couple of hours — I tear up.

Is this all because of a man I've met twice?

Totally ridiculous. What is wrong with me?

Or is this because of Kerri's opinion, that Matteo somehow thinks that we're soul mates? The very thought thrills and shocks me. Actually, it scares the crap out of me, because I know that if I did become a vampire and find my soul mate, then eventually I'd have to return to being mortal.

All I want is to be immortal. I don't even really want a man in my life, just a vampire who will turn me. That Matteo was gorgeous and sexy and a perfect candidate to pop my proverbial virginal cherry... well, that was a feature, not a bug.

I didn't question Kerri further about her opinion because the idea seems stupid, the more I think about it. Matteo seemed too pissed at me when he told me to leave. That's not the behavior of a guy who just met his soul mate.

Finally, on Wednesday, I rally for psych class. It's like I'm genetically incapable of blowing off days of lectures. I know plenty of people do, but even in my foul mood and feverish state, I can't let myself sink that far. Plus the nagging voice of my mother echoes in my head, the one that tells me I need to work hard and graduate at the top of my class.

You need to impress your medical school professors before you even set foot on the campus, Mom says. So much fucking pressure to do everything right now. If I were immortal, I wouldn't feel that urge to overachieve.

"You sure you're okay? Maybe you should stay home another day." Kerri says, as I pull on an all-black ensemble. I realize that it's the sweater I wore to Matteo's, and his faint scent hits my nose.

"Dammit."

"What?"

"It smells like him. Fuck this." I strip off the sweater and open a drawer, pawing around for a turtleneck.

Kerri sighs. "I'm sorry."

I pull the turtleneck over my head and shrug on my jacket. "Not your fault. I'll see you later. I'm going to grab a coffee and a muffin at the cafeteria before class. Or try to."

"Okay, but don't feel bad if you have to come back."

I give her a little wave and shuffle out of the room. It's the first time I've left in three days, and all around me, there are signs of life and sunshine, of bubbly, laughing students and a bright spring day.

Dammit, I wish I'd brought my sunglasses.

Somehow I manage to leave the dorm building and cross the street. I almost turn around when I see the coffee line, but stand there with a sigh and a sour face until I fill a small cup. I locate a blueberry muffin and head to the cashier.

When I get to the register, I paw around in my purse for my meal card. The employee gives me a withering stare, and a guy behind me taps his foot. "Uh, crap. I uh, can't find it. I live across the street in room two-oh-four, um. Wait."

"Here. Put it on mine. I have a coffee." The guy behind me reaches around to hand the cashier his meal card.

"Uh, thanks." I blink at him while shoving my wallet back into the purse.

The guy's cute, tall with white blond spiky hair and giant blue eyes. Weird. I've never seen him before.

"Thanks, I owe you one." This is the first time I've smiled in days.

"I'll take you up on that." He swaggers away, and I notice he's wearing jeans, red Docs and a grey Henley.

I walk to the stairs that will take me to psych class, feeling a little better about humanity. Although I need to find my meal card; without it, I can't eat. There's no way I can rely on Kerri to bring me food three times a day, and I don't make enough in my part time work-study job to buy food at restaurants every meal.

I settle into class, arranging my coffee, the muffin, my pen and a notebook on the desk in front of me. Purposefully I came early, so I could eat in peace before class. There are a couple of other people in the room, drinking coffee and reviewing notes.

Again, I look through my bag, hoping the meal card will turn up. I've lost it twice before, and it will be a hundred bucks to replace — an amount I'd have to get from Mom, which is the last thing I want right now. She'll surely call me irresponsible and forgetful.

I search in every pocket in my bag, and even flip through a small notebook, wondering if it wedged in there somehow.

Then I recall how my bag spilled open at Matteo's, and groan aloud. I probably left it at his house, along with the charred remains of my favorite bra and my dignity.

"Fuck," I whisper, my shoulders sagging. Exhaustion washes over me.

A girl in front of me turns and glares.

"Sorry," I whisper.

Printed by BoD™in Norderstedt, Germany